# THE
# MADNESS
## OF
# HISTORY

⋈

N. J. DODIC

1994

Exile Editions
TORONTO

Text Copyright
© N. J. Dodic,
1994

Copyright
© Exile Editions Limited,
1994

•

FIRST PRINTING

•

This Edition is published by Exile Editions Limited,
20 Dale Avenue, Toronto, Ontario, Canada M4W 1K4

Sales Distribution
General Publishing Co. Ltd.,
30 Lesmill Road, Don Mills, Ontario M3B 2T6

•

Design by MICHAEL P. CALLAGHAN
Typeset by MOONS OF JUPITER
Printed by BEST BOOK MANUFACTURERS
Cover CGI by MICHAEL P. CALLAGHAN
Author's photo by JOHN REEVES

The author wishes to thank
the Ontario Arts Council for its support.

The publisher wishes to acknowledge
the assistance towards publication
of the Canada Council, the Ontario Arts Council,
and the Ministry of Culture, Tourism, & Recreation.

ISBN 1-55096-0644

*for my parents*

⋈

# 1

I'm not Joan of Arc, my skin crackling beneath the voluptuous flames.

I'm not Anne Frank, my sunken eyes seeking answers in the faces of ghosts who stumble about me, our destination ashes.

I'm not Eva Braun, my fat heart poisoned and then burned in the garden above the bunker.

And I'm not Sylvia Plath, overwhelmed by my own breathing and understood by no one and I like my head well done.

No, I'm only Mara Rustic, but consider my weakness for hyperbole when I say that I suffer the same awful heat. Autumn in Toronto is a liar of a season. I walk home from the bookstore, through the park and then along the deserted narrow footpath to Chester Avenue. The warm wind hits me from above, and then from another direction, cool. Then no breeze at all, only the gentle waving of orange and lemon-yellow leaves high up in the ancient oak trees.

The tenement building stands on the corner, nine stories tall, the elevator broken six months now and me living on the top floor. A tough call, whether or not to complain. All that movement and effort and face-to-face.

I peer into my mail slot, and lift out a white envelope. I study the thing, five-and-a-quarter by seven-and-a-quarter inches, an estimate. It may be a birthday card from my uncle; tomorrow I turn twenty-eight. The postmark reads BEOGRAD, but I can't imagine Nick going back to the Old World, even in peacetime.

My feet creak the wooden stairs up to my one-bedroom apartment. The main room is furnished with a chair, a writing table and a shelf holding a few art books, surrealists mostly. Dali's landscapes, brown-scorched earth and peacock-blue skies, deliver me always to strange places.

I fall into a chair, a black recliner that once sat abandoned in the hallway. A wind knocks rickety branches against the windowpane. Outside, the sounds of children playing, laughing, fighting and I'm telling Mommy.

Here in my chair I drag a knife along the edge of the mystery envelope. The paper is thin. The knife is sharp. My humor is low.

✖

One minute later. All of yesterday's riddles, nightmares and lullabies spill from the smeared mouth of a devil/clown giving his deathbed confession.

⋈

# 2

I first felt that my parents did not love one another on July 20th, 1969. *Life Magazine*, helpfully enough, pinpoints it to 10:56 a.m., Eastern Daylight Time. Of course, *Life* wasn't documenting the domestic troubles of Anthony Rustic and his wife Jelina, but rather the red, white and blue heroics of Neil Armstrong and the rest of the Apollo XI crew.

I was a four-and-a-half-year-old girl, kneeling in front of a black and white television set, tugging at my pajamas. The spaceship landed, and the picture skipped up and down before righting itself. I jumped up and clapped and shouted, "The moon! The moon! The moon!"

Spinning away from the set, I turned to my parents. My father's face was blank, uncomplicated by lunar thoughts. He'd been home since seven-thirty from his night watchman's job, sleeping on the couch. I asked him once why he dozed on the couch when his long legs didn't fit. "It's bad luck to lie in bed when the sun's up," he said.

My mother pulled a maroon sweater over her head. Beneath her sad eyes, weary pouches of skin added years to her twenty-nine. The cotton sweater and black skirt, her workwear, indicated she would soon be on a streetcar, the red rocket scraping along King Street with my hand-wringing mother on her way to scrub the sinks and toilets of some family in

Rosedale. She was looking for something in her purse, a comb, her three-inch wooden Virgin, something, and I guessed then, seconds after the Americans had landed and probably during Neil's One Small Step speech, that my immigrant parents' lives were loveless.

Mama put her hands to her mouth and ran to the bathroom. I heard vomit hitting still water, a handful of pebbles dropped in a pond. Two mornings in a row.

My father yawned, and I turned the television off.

✖

# 3

"Look at the holes in your dress, Mara. A pretty girl should have a pretty dress. Boys will run away when they see this." Mrs. Pontich patted my head.

I gazed gloomily at my feet. "I don't want boys to like me. I like girls."

"Oh Mara, you just wait and see."

"See what?"

"You'll see."

I hated her ham-eating face, and her hands, those sausage fingers, each massive arm weighing more than me. I hated her cruel putdowns of my mother. As we walked down the front porch steps of the four-bedroom Pontich bungalow, I couldn't wait to tell my mother what I thought of the evil woman.

"Shut up, girl," my mother hissed. "Olga looks out for us. She begged Danilo to give your father a job."

My mother, for the tenth time, explained that Mr. Pontich worked as a supervisor at the Mattel toy factory, and that he recommended my father for the night watchman's job.

"And besides," she added, looking through the rain to see if the Islington bus was approaching, "it's because your father works at Mattel that you have all those dolls. More dolls than a princess, I would think."

It was true. My father, doing his rounds, would happen upon giant garbage bins where all the irregular toys were discarded. Once, he brought home three identical dolls and left them at the foot of my bed for me to see when I awoke. The dolls had straight, grim lips, snub noses and cheekbones framed by long blonde hairs. They had no eyes. Instead, there were dark tunnels burrowed into the back of the dolls' plastic heads. They spoke to me in squeaky, plaintive voices: "Mara, Mara, Mara, they took out our eyes! My God, they took out our eyes!"

When we got home, my father, lying on the couch, sat up and asked us how cookies and Turkish coffee with Mrs. Pontich had gone.

"Fine," my mother sighed, unbuttoning her grey overcoat.

My father caught me scowling. "What about you, Mače? Did you have a good time?"

"Don't ask her anything," my mother cut in. She ran both hands through her hair and let it fall behind her like a wet mop. "Mara's becoming a critic."

My father rubbed the back of his neck and grumbled, "If she doesn't like Olga, it's for a reason."

"What's that supposed to mean?"

My father shrugged and said, "Animals and children have instincts about bad people."

"Olga's not a bad woman," my mother said, astonished and offended.

"Come on. She's a witch."

My mother flung her coat to the floor. "In front of the girl. Fine, fine, wonderful. Nice lesson to teach your daughter." Then to me, full of reproach: "Go to your room!"

In bed, counting paint chips in the ceiling, I heard them yelling until my mother's voice broke.

She began to cry, and my father apologized, said he forgot how close she was, did she feel alright, sorry, sorry, sorry.

¤

Two days before Christmas, my mother and I bumped into Mrs. Pontich at the supermarket. She invited us to her home. My mother said it was getting late, she was tired, she had to cook dinner. But Mrs. Pontich, that perfumed bully, she knew how to push people (even I knew her tricks), and together we forged our way to her home, our bodies bent against the wind and the snow and my brother less than a week away.

She led us to the room she'd said would someday be her baby's. I recalled being in the room a few months earlier: empty, all echoes; it gave me a chill. Now, only warmth, a lush, pink carpet cushioning our feet, and candy-cane wallpaper hugging the walls.

In the middle of this, a huge crib that looked, even smelled, brand new. A mobile dangled above the crib, putting in motion blue bunnies and fairy chimes. Inside the crib, two teddy bears sat leaning against one another, one brown, one white, both smiling. They were glamorous as movie stars.

"I'm expecting," Mrs. Pontich announced, gripping her gut with pride.

"Expecting what?" my mother asked.

"A baby, what else? We've been sending cards back home all week."

My mother nodded. Her hands clutched the crib. It was big enough for five babies. It was big enough for Mrs. Pontich.

"Lovely, isn't it?" the evil woman chuckled. "Too bad *your* baby won't see this kind of luxury."

My mother's eyes got glassy. She found my hand and pulled me from the room, through the hallway and out the front door.

Behind us, Mrs. Pontich's voice rang out: "Where are you going? Jelina, I was kidding! Come back, the coffee's ready. Jelina!"

Six days later, Danny was born.

⋈

# 4

Valerie, in my kindergarten class, told me to watch the moon that night. She said it would be full and that scary things happened under a full moon. We lived on the third floor of a four-storey walk-up, and from my bedroom window I had a clear, panoramic view of the street. That night, however, the world lay obscured by a thick fog, rolling in waves. The moon came out for a second, a vampire smirk shining its bloodless light on me. It was a school night and I should have been in bed, but I wanted to see what Valerie meant. My feet felt cold on the bare floor.

And all at once I saw her. I didn't know it was her then, but I saw her. She appeared from nowhere, from shadows, maybe from the main entrance downstairs. She had her back to me and the fog camouflaged her, she carried it with her as she went. I couldn't tell if she was walking. My eyes strained to see, but beneath her blue flowing robe I saw no feet, no shoes. My heart beat fast. I pressed my nose to the window. A cream-colored hood covered her head and she wouldn't turn around. The fog, the dead silence, the way she floated, made me feel her shame. She was fading, and I called out —

"Mara!"

Who?

"Mara, what are you doing awake? Tomorrow's school." My father, set for work, held a paper bag with his tuna sandwiches in it.

"Sorry." I climbed back into bed.

"You apologize too much," he said. "No one believes you. Go to sleep, don't bother your mother in the morning. She has visitors in her head."

I asked him what he meant.

He gave me a never-mind shake of the head and said, "I'm going."

"Tata?"

"What?"

I pointed to a book on the dresser. "Read to me?"

My father winced. He picked up the book. "Who gave you this?"

"Miss Henderson showed us how to take them out of the library."

"You can read?"

"Yeah, but I don't know all the words yet."

"Of course you don't."

We looked at each other. "Will you read to me, Tata?"

"Your mother likes to read to you. Ask her."

"She only reads the Bible to me."

He bit his bottom lip. "Nothing wrong with that."

"Please, Tata. Just a little."

He sucked in half the air in the room. "Sorry, Mače. No time."

The wide skull of the moon winked at me.

My father stood in the doorway, his blue polyester uniform making him sweat, his chin resting somberly on his chest. "What if I tell you a story?"

"Okay, Tata." I pushed my pillow back and sat up.

"It'll have to be quick, though."

"Do you know Goldilocks?   That's my favorite."

"No. No, I don't."

"How about Little Red Riding Hood?"

"Never heard of it."

"The Little Engine That Could?"

"No."  He took off his cap and sat on the edge of the bed.  The mattress sank, and I shifted over to keep from sliding.  "You know what war is, right?"

"Like when the men on t.v. shoot everything?"

"Okay, but what you see on t.v. is people makebelieving war.  None of it's true.  This story's about a little boy — "

"How old?"

"Twelve.  And this boy wants to be friends with these older boys — "

"Why?"

"I don't know, he just does.  I have to go to work soon, so shut up."

"Sorry."

"Anyway, these older boys like to smoke.  They tell the boy that they'll take him into their group if he gets them a pack of cigarettes.  The boy asks, 'How do I do that?  The Nazis have all the cigarettes.'"

"What're Nazis?"

"What?"

"Nazis.  What're Nazis?"

"Oh, they were the soldiers who invaded the village.  Bad guys.  So this boy — "

"Tata?"

"What?  What?"

"Are you the boy in the story?"

An exasperated smile, he cupped his hand on my cheek so tenderly, like a lover.  "You know, your mother's right, you're a *djevojka detektiv*."

"I'm not."

"Listen, I have to go to work — "

"No, please, no.  Finish the story.  The little boy's trying to get cigarettes for the older boys."

"Alright, alright.  Close your eyes.  Good. Now, the boy decides to do something very foolish. He makes plans to steal a pack of cigarettes from a red-headed soldier guarding a barn."

"Why was he guarding a barn?"

"I don't know, maybe the cows were up to something.  Close your eyes.  The boy watches the soldier tip forward his helmet to shield his eyes from the sun.  The soldier's leaning in a lazy sort of way, and the boy can tell he's fallen asleep.  The boy tiptoes toward the soldier.  He spies the sharp corners of a pack of cigarettes poking out from the soldier's shirt pocket.  The boy bends down, too stupid to be frightened, and he undoes the snap on the pocket.  He has the cigarette pack lifted almost all the way out when the soldier wakes up with a start.  The boy grabs the cigarettes and runs."

He rapid-tapped two fingers on my forearm to simulate a running boy.

"Behind him, the soldier scrambles to his feet screaming ugly German words.  But the boy doesn't care, the boy's laughing out loud, he knows his legs are young and strong and he knows that soldiers are too dignified to chase after little children.  What the boy doesn't know, you see, is what's in the heart of a Nazi soldier.  Three bullets — three bullets! — whistle past the boy's ears, and, though he doesn't stop running, he does stop laughing.  He gets away unharmed, and he throws the cigarettes down a well."

He paused, to see if I was still awake.

"When the older boys caught up to him, he told them he didn't need friends like them.  And the story doesn't end there.  Two or three days later, the boy learned that one of his school chums had been shot dead by a red-headed Nazi.  For stealing his cig-arettes.  This friend, he didn't even look like the boy, he was much shorter, he was even fat, what with his father being a pastry chef.  Still, it was the friend who got killed."

He stopped.

I opened my eyes.

He must have figured out that I wanted more, a proper ending, a moral like in the stories from school.  "Luck," he explained.

Simple.

✕

# 5

Darkness lingered malevolently into the morning. I'd had another dream about the dolls, and I'd been awake the whole night praying for the sun to rise. So I heard my father when he opened the whining front door, when he kicked his shoes off, and when he went in to check on Danny in his makeshift crib.

"You're up early, Jelina."

"Someone has to feed the baby. Put that cigarette out."

My father cleared his throat. "I talked to Danilo Pontich today."

A gasp from my mother. "Don't tell me you lost your job."

"No, it's not that." He coughed. "It's Olga. She's had a miscarriage."

A quiet moment.

Then a giggle. And laughter. Full-blown, dangerous laughter.

My father's head exploded. "Jelina! What, are you crazy? Quiet! Please, be quiet. Please! You're going to wake Mara!"

¤

# 6

The mirror I'm looking into is cracked in the upper left-hand corner. The frame is plastic painted black, so you can't tell how cheap it is until you touch it. I bought it at a yard sale years ago. The wobbly-eyed old man who sold it to me lied about how much he paid for it, and he wouldn't acknowledge the crack.

"How much?" I asked.

He blinked twice and said, "The prince of a foreign country once combed his cascading blonde locks by the unerring reflection this mirror provided."

"Which prince?"

He licked his dry lips. "He's dead now."

We eventually settled on eleven dollars.

Now, the reflection my mirror gives, contrary to previous information, is perpetually hazy. If you look into it late at night, with one candle burning dust, the effect is dream-like. I haven't any candles right now, but it doesn't matter.

The top of me is five-and-a-half feet off the ground. My head's large for my body. Hair black, short, straight-banged and borderline greasy, it causes me to be mistaken alternately for a vagrant or a disaffected art student.

Eyes, brown. My mother used to call them detective eyes, sneaking around where they shouldn't.

A lover once told me they move furtively, charting possible escape routes (he exaggerated; he was a poet). And scattered in the white of my right eye are dark pigmentation dots, something I've yet to see in anyone else, but no, it probably doesn't mean anything.

Hanging between my eyes is a somewhat oversized nose that hints at my Serbian side. A fleshy nose, a meaty nose, a real presence.

Cheekbones, high. My first Hallowe'en, my father attached crow feathers to my hair and dabbed red Indian war paint from Woolco on my ruddy cheeks; he pretended to be afraid for his scalp.

Lips, full. A detriment when I was younger (playground teasing), but now they're in vogue, sensuous all of a sudden. No lipstick, though; that'd be too sarcastic, even for me.

Arms and shoulders, slender. But deceptively strong, I swim sometimes. A strange, knobby bone protrudes from both my wrists. My mother told me a babysitter dropped me. My parents could never afford a babysitter.

Breasts, small. But I've received compliments, it's true, "pert," etc.

My stomach's getting kind of soft and lumpy, beginning to show age. Maybe that should bother me. It doesn't.

Above my vagina, a thick patch of hair curls into black knots. Most of my lovers say it looks natural, sexy even (or at least they used to, back then).

My ass is round, nice to sit on, sort of disproportionate. My hips, too. Never could figure how I've always been thin, you know, slim waist, but have this chunky ass and wide-mother hips. The dreaded child-bearing years are upon me, now that's a bad joke.

I'm rambling, that's a given, something I will give you, but let me ask: Which is the more tangible, a memory or a photograph?  The only picture I have of me with my parents was taken the day my mother's friend Dinka got married.  The three of us are standing in someone's garden, a grapevine curling opulently in the background.  My father looks elegant in a dark suit and tie, my mother pretty in a white jacket with big black buttons.  Me, I'm in front, centred, maybe three years old, wearing a white dress with matching tights.  No one's touching anyone, no one's smiling.  The sun is behind us, and we all have shadows for eyes.

It's the only picture I have of them, and I can't remember a thing about that day.

⋈

# 7

The sleep in my eyes eclipsed my vision, no moon on, I had to pat the walls to get to the bathroom.  As I closed my hand around the doorknob, I felt someone's breath warm the back of my neck.

I peeked over my shoulder. Nothing.

No, a moan, miles away.  Beneath the door to my parents' room a puff of mist.  My bare feet made sucking sounds on the floor, in each step a whisper echoed.  The door leaned menacingly to the left, swaying, as if dancing a slow dance.  I nudged it open.  Vapors of hot air stung my face, distilling the stench of rotting flesh.  The room was dark and heavy as the inside of a coffin.  But I had flashlights for eyes.

To my right, Danny lay in his crib, pacifier in mouth, his hair matted down with perspiration.  Six black flies flew circles above his head.

I beamed to the bed.  My father was on top. Shed of his clothing, he seemed younger, boyish.  His buttocks rose and fell into a pair of parted legs.

I walked closer, came upon them in their embrace, an arm's length away.  The smell of them, the reek of an eternity.  Balls of sweat slid down my father's back.  A white breast flopped to the side, the other cupped in my father's hand.

I moved to the headboard.  My mother's eyes were shut tight against her own death.  Without speaking I said, *Read to me, Mama, about your living dogs and dead lions*, and her eyelids eased open. Her eyes held mine and refused to let go. Tears mixed with sweat, streamed past her ears, she wanted mercy but wouldn't let me look away. He pushed harder and harder, one more brute thrust and he collapsed on her.

She brought her hand to her mouth and gazed at the far wall, where a plastic Jesus hung with head bowed, hands and feet glued to the cross.

My flashlights flickered, failed, then came back on.

My father, inhaling and exhaling, rolled off her, onto his back and nearer to me, introducing me to the male organ, his serpent long and fat, the tip blood-rushed and beating like a mini-heart and my hand, I wanted to touch it, but no, Mama lying there crying and me growing bigger and bigger filling the room had to get out before the batteries in my flashlights and the whispers...

⊐⊏

# 8

"Little Mara with the big nose, get on your knees and smell my toes."

He followed me from the sandbox to the swings. I backed into a seat, stuttered three steps and pushed myself into flight. "Go away," I said.

The earth lay waiting for rain. The pale-green leaves of maple trees trembled in the faint wind. Justin Eton-Edwards, a large orange-haired boy from my class, hit me from behind.

His mother ("Mummy") shared a park bench with my parents. Words erupted from her like stampeding buffalo, loud and burly, tumbling over one another. Having made the aquaintance of Mr. and Mrs. Rustic, she found herself enjoying a pleasant, if one-sided, conversation:

"The diversity of people here in Toronto, why, from Justin's class, there's you two from Yugoslavia, the Chans from Hong Kong, all the Italian immigrants and, I mean, just the sheer diversity, and — Justin, play nice — oh yes, I've never met anyone from South America, have you?"

My father sat between the women, a cigarette in his mouth, one eye squinting the smoke. My mother's arm, a slow-moving piston, rocked Danny's carriage. She watched me while listenening to Mrs. Eton-Edwards.

Suddenly the woman was howling at a joke she'd told. My father looked quizzically at my mother. Neither understood what possessed this woman, this babbling machine-gun whose English accent and turquoise eye-shadow relegated them both to some black and white nether world.

"What are you looking at your mummy for?"

"What?"

Justin punched me hard in the back of the head. I tucked my legs in, straightened them out, and swung higher. He walked to the front of the swing and stood close to where my feet came up on the incline, defying me to hit him. "How come girls in Canada are so ugly?" he asked, tossing sand onto my skirt.

"Please don't throw that at me."

"Okay." He threw more.

My feet dragged the ground and I hopped off the swing. I began to walk towards my mother, but Justin grabbed me and pulled me back. He slapped me on the nose and I fell.

I stood up. Mrs. Eton-Edwards was laughing again, Justin had a fistful of my hair, he was tugging it and wouldn't let go. He kept pulling and pushing and I reached for the swing, chain rattling revenge, the metal edge jutting out of the seat, and I drove it into his temple. Blood trickled down his cheek and he staggered, raised an eyebrow at me and didn't say anything, not even ouch. His mother came running, very fast in her pumps, and carried him off like an old suitcase whose handle had broken. I watched them get into a blue station wagon, recede into the distance, and vanish.

The crunching rumble of carriage wheels on gravel transformed any regret into fear. I decided against running; I would wait. My parents had never spanked me in public before. Of course, I'd never attempted murder before. I lowered my head, and raindrops kissed my shoulders.

My mother put her arm around me. "What took you so long, Mara? The orange bastard had it coming."

My father lit a fresh cigarette. "Let's go home."

⋈

# 9

A snowfall greeted Danny's first birthday. My mother had planned a party for him, and Danny and I waited in my bedroom. He lay on his back, sucking his fingers and sweating. Danny sweated all the time — when he slept, when he ate, when he crawled to my room towing his milk bottle behind him. My father would nod and call it a good sign, saying that sweaty babies grew up to be lawyers.

I wiped Danny's forehead with a damp cloth. He slid two spit-covered fingers from his mouth and glanced up at me with lips parted and tiny tongue sitting still. His eyes, big and clear, reflected the bare light bulb hanging from the ceiling. The yellow bulb blistered the Sahara sun, his were the mournful eyes of a camel forsaken in the desert.

My mother was baking a chocolate cake, her radio tuned to the station that played Macedonian music for one hour every Saturday. I could make out the song, it was one I'd heard before, with two men singing and making fun of each other's wives (one's ugly, the other can't cook). In the background there was an accordion, a mandolin and some bleating. What I liked best was the animal sounds, often sheep, but also riled-up dogs and braying donkeys. The cows were my favorite, a bass choir of mooing accompanied by clanking bells.

My mother never missed the program, maybe because the songs made her think about her childhood. She was born in Macedonia in a village just south of Skopje, where a hairless aunt had taught her to play a wooden flute. This much my father imparted to me, since my mother hated to speak of the past.

Late one evening, however, in the middle of reading the story of Ruth to me, she closed the Bible and laid it on her lap beside her wooden Virgin. "I'm going to tell you about my Tetka Zlatica."

I had to shake myself awake, I'd already begun my astronaut dream, going to the moon. "Your bald aunt."

She looked surprised. "Yes, Zlatica was bald."

She sat up in her chair. Save for the low, comforting drone of the odd car passing beyond the window, the night was serenely devoid of commotion.

"Zlatica was beautiful," she began. "She didn't need hair. She was tall, the tallest woman in the village, and she had the strongest nose, by far. And her cheekbones, they were almost as pretty as yours, Mara."

"Mine aren't so pretty."

"Sure they are. Not that it matters. The point is, Tetka Zlatica — "

"Is she dead?"

My mother looked at me like I was out of focus. "What are you, a gravedigger?"

"So, she is dead."

"No," she said. "What did you see on t.v. today?"

"Nothing."

"What a question: 'Is she dead?'"

"Sorry."

"No need to be sorry. We're just talking. Like a mother and daughter."

"Will she ever come visit us?" I asked.

"No."  The edges of her mouth tightened, and wistfulness crept into her tone.  "It's strange, Mara."

"What is?"

"Well, Zlatica was always bald, even as a young girl.  Because no man wanted her, she was free to do what she liked."

"I don't understand."

She stood up, drew the curtains, and sat down again.  She told me her aunt was the happiest woman she'd ever known, always dancing and singing, making songs up.  Zlatica used to sneak her candy bars that tasted like pieces of heaven, and no one was supposed to know because chocolate was so hard to come by in Yugoslavia after the war.  When she was sixteen, her family packed up and moved to Serbia, leaving her aunt and baby brother behind.  Her mother made her exchange her flute for a pair of shoes, and she cried for three days.  After telling me all this, my mother sang to me, for the first time, a lullaby Tetka Zlatica taught her:

> *Mala kuća kamena*
> *sa tri mala prozora,*
> *zeleni im kapci,*
> *i krov sav od plamena,*
> *a na krovu vrapci.*

The melody was sweet and lilting, my mother's voice thin, faraway and eerie:

> A little house of stone
> with three little windows,
> green their shutters,
> and the roof all aflame,
> and on the roof, sparrows.

She asked if I'd like to learn how to make *palicinke*. I said okay, and she said goodnight and left me. I spent the night singing the song in my head.

⋈

My mother switched off the radio. "Mara, your friend is here!"

I ran downstairs to meet Valerie.

"Hi."

"Hi." She handed me a box wrapped in blue paper. "For Danny."

"What is it?"

"Who knows."

Valerie pulled her coat, hat and mittens off. I helped her with her boots.

"Hello, Mrs. Rustic," Valerie said. She tapped the box. "This is Danny's present."

"Oh, that's nice. Thank your mother for me."

Valerie and I went to my room. We looked at Danny, lying on his back and wagging his limbs like a turned-over turtle. "Your brother sweats a lot."

"Yeah."

She sat on the bed beside Danny. "Get any toys for Christmas?"

"Not really."

She shrugged. "Your brother really sweats a lot."

"Yeah."

She stretched out and put her feet up on the bed. "What kind of cake is your mom making?"

"Chocolate."

She wiped her nose with the back of her hand. "Cartoons?"

"Okay."

My father was sleeping on the couch, so we watched Bugs Bunny with the volume turned down. During a commercial, I asked Valerie, "Which character do you like best?"

"I don't know. Bugs, I guess. Or maybe that fat rooster, whatever his name is. I guess you like Roadrunner."

"Yeah."

My mother's voice from the kitchen: "Cake's ready."

My father sprang up from the couch and rushed to the bathroom.

My mother had been ebullient all week, making decisions on the food for Danny's birthday party, what toys to buy him, even getting my father to borrow Mr. Pontich's camera.

My father emerged from the bathroom sporting a rubber nose and a polka-dot shirt, lipstick smeared all over his mouth, topped off by a fuzzy red wig. He goose-stepped around the room and did a pratfall, and Valerie and I laughed. My mother lowered Danny into his high-chair and told me to light the big purple candle on the cake. I did, and then I carried the cake toward the table. "Be careful," my mother said.

It wasn't a very big cake. I dropped it. It landed upside down, icing on the linoleum floor and the candle broken in two. Everyone was quiet, except for Danny, who giggled.

My mother gritted her teeth. My father said, "Jelina, it was an accident," but she didn't hear anything, her eyes were popping, she went berserk.

"You little monster! You're jealous of your brother, eh? What do you do to him when no one's watching?"

My father ripped off the wig and said, "Leave her alone. She's a child."

With stunning speed, my mother scratched him, leaving four lines of blood on his cheek. He reached out to her. She shoved me at him. I lost my balance on the icing and landed at his feet.

"Stop it!" my father pleaded, hooking me up by my armpits as my mother picked a saucer up from the sink and whirled it at him; it shattered against the wall like a crisp gunshot. Valerie slipped away, swift as a cat in danger. My father threw up his arms, but the second saucer bruised him below the eye.

Danny gurgled in a peculiar way, and my mother lunged at him, my father and I open-mouthed statues, gaping as her fingers crushed his throat with all her mad energy. My father leapt into life and I went to help and we unclenched her fingers one by one and the back of my father's hand struck her with such impact that she crumpled to the floor and let out a groan.

Danny was burping for air, my father whisked him to the bathroom.

I sat down beside her. Her belly swelled with her breathing, and she'd begun to sob. I stroked her hair; it felt soft, and smelled like lilacs.

"I'm sorry, Mama."

She lay on her side, eyes closed, face pinched against the linoleum floor. "I know, darling. I know."

☒

Later that night my father roused my mother from her sleep and told her to take two pills, that she'd feel better.

Then he came and eased Danny from my arms. "I'll put him in his crib." He looked worn out, his cheek scabbed red and some lipstick still on his mouth.  He sat on my bed.

"What's going to happen, Tata?"

"Your father's a stupid man, Mače."

"No."

"I can barely read or write."

I started crying.

"Don't be sad," he said, and now he was crying, too.

"Tata?"

"Shh."  He leaned over and kissed my forehead, and then he got up slowly and backed out of the room.

⋈

For hours I couldn't sleep, tossing into dream after dream, dark images flitting before my eyes.  But I fell asleep, I must have, because a voice, a female voice, awakened me.

She stood at the foot of my bed in her blue robe, her head bowed, her back to me.  She was saying something, murmuring, a violent incantation building in intensity until her left arm came up, finger pointing at the window.

I leapt out of bed and looked down to where a taxi waited in the street, to my father, breath visible in the winter air, duffel bag swinging off one arm, the other pressing a bundled-up Danny to his chest.

I ran down the staircase, two, three steps at a time.

The taxi accelerated, and losing ground I screamed, "No, Tata, no!"

My father spun around in the back seat and looked out the rear window.

I kept running, cold air filling my lungs, icicles stuck in the corners of my eyes.  The taxi disappeared.

My heart burst, and I faded in the bosom of a warm snowbank.

✕

She was there, waiting.  My eyes were level with her feet, naked as mine.  I wiped the tears away, and she held my hand and walked me back to my room.

She let me see her face.

⋈

# 10

*21 Oktobar*

*Dear Miss Rustić,*

*Forgive me my English, I was told you might not read very well Srpski so I am trying to do best with my dictionary. My name is Zivko Pavić, and I am a lawyer from Beograd. It is unfortunate to tell you that your father and my friend, Tony Rustic, died on 7 July. I am sorry for your loss.*

*I also am sorry for not contacting you sooner, but you were not easy to find and no telefon number, said operator in Toronto.*

*In my possession is things your father wanted you to have, but before sending I need to hear from your situation on these matters.*

*Please call me or write to me. My numbers are on my business card, enclosed.*

*Sincerely,*

*Zivko Pavić*

⋈

# 11

September 6, 1980.

Everything in my life is so strange, if I don't write it down I'll go crazy.  Last Monday, ten days after Mama died, I awoke to loud knocking at the front door.  I thought someone had the wrong address, since all the mourners had stopped nosing around, Mama's friend Dinka had finally listened to me and moved out.  She's a nice woman, but I can take better care of myself than someone who loses her dentures once a day, plus all her bawling!  Even her dog looks depressed.

Anyway, the knocking.  I tumbled out of bed, opened the front door and saw a dark-haired man standing there.  He brushed past me, wheeling a black suitcase in from the hallway, ramming it against the wall behind the door.  He turned around, but he didn't look at me.  His head, a regular turret, rotated slowly on his shoulders, surveying everything around him.

He wore a long brown suede coat and looked to be about twenty-five years old.  I'd never seen him before, he had the kind of brooding face and thick eyebrows you don't forget.  He was sniffing the air and, after a few seconds, it dawned on me that I was still in my pajamas with this man in my living room. I stepped away.

"Mara, right?" he said, closing the door.

"Who are you?"

He held his hand out to me, said, "I'm Nick," and still wouldn't make eye contact. I shook his clammy hand (but only briefly, as he lost interest right away).

"Pleased to meet you."

"Sure, kid."

A quiet moment. Then I asked, as politely as I could, "Who are you?"

His head tilted to one side, which I took to mean he thought my question was stupid. He scratched his elbow, sniffed some more and said, "I'm Nick! Your uncle, for God's sake! From Yugoslavia, for God's sake!"

I nodded. "Oh."

"Well?"

I rushed my brain and remembered that Mama did once mention a baby brother, the one Tetka Zlatica raised when the family moved to Serbia.

He flopped on the couch like a tired, grouchy octopus. "Get the letter?"

"Letter? No."

"I got one."

He didn't elaborate. I didn't know what to say next. As he spoke English with no accent, I said, real casually, "So, Nick, you speak English very well."

"So do you, kid," he said.

I sat down next to him. "I really don't know what this is all about."

He looked me in the eye, finally. His eyes were the color of elephants, just like Mama's, big and grey, I could actually see her in him. He said, "It's a long story." And then he added, sort of priest-like, "I'm sorry about Jelina. Your mother loved you very much."

My heart raced a little when I heard that. None of Mama's friends — not even any of my friends — had said anything half as comforting. "You talked to her? She told you she loved me?"

He looked away again. "Naw. Just a feeling. Whatever." He looked at his watch. "Where's the bathroom in this place?"

That was four days ago. Nick is not normal. I don't think I like him, and I'll probably hate him once I figure him out, but at least he's not crying all over the place like Dinka, that lawn sprinkler with bracelets.

He acts like he's the king of me. He goes to the grocery store and buys food that I'm supposed to cook for both of us, and I do, not because I'm a girl but because he paid for it and I have to do my share. One day I made burgers for him, and all the punk could do was pick at the meat and say, "Shameful." Then he pushed the plate away, like the thing was contagious or something.

I got mad. "What are you saying, that my cooking stinks?"

He tipped his chin up at the plate. "Smell for yourself, kid."

I know he doesn't want to be here. I'm not sure why he is, but someone, probably Dinka, called up Tetka Zlatica in Macedonia and told her what happened to Mama. I think Zlatica may have wanted to take care of me herself, only she's eighty years old and can't get around very well, which is too bad because I'd love to meet her (and to never have met Nick). She raised Nick, and I guess he has to do whatever she says, because he was living in Belgrade, making it big in a rock band (he says) when Tetka Zlatica wrote him and told him to go to Canada to look after me. And now here he is, making faces at me over my cooking. What a jerk! I wish people'd just leave me alone. I'm not yet sixteen, but it feels like I'm much older. I have the summer job at the bookstore, and I could work full-time if I had to. I can take care of myself. Of course, what I should be doing is worrying about money. Speaking of which, Nick gave me some yesterday for school supplies, which was nice of him. Still, I can't help hating him for sleeping in my parents' bed. Am I weird?

¤

September 7.

Just before Mama died, I transferred to an "alternative" school called Raoul Wallenberg, named after the hero who saved so many Jews in World War Two. The school's downtown, Spadina and Bloor, so I have to take the subway (nine stops, but I don't mind). Within one block of Wallenberg there're six bookstores, ten cafés and The Bloor Cinema with its great old movies.

I hated technical school. Mama wanted me to get a practical education, stuff like sewing and cooking, as well as "boy" things like auto repair and carpentry. But all I wanted to do was read, especially poetry. I remember in grade five, Mrs. Taylor, with the booming, theatrical delivery, got me hooked when she would read from Tennyson and Wordsworth and Dylan Thomas. Then I started signing out poetry books from the library and reading them out loud in bed. Once Mama heard me from her bedroom and sort of freaked, thinking demons had invaded me like the goop-retching girl in *The Exorcist*.

My favourites right now are Sylvia Plath and Stevie Smith. I like Leonard Cohen, too, I took out one of his records. He has this amazing song, "Who By Fire," where he lists off all these ways to die, fire, water, avalanche, etc. When the chorus comes up he gets formal, like a rich man's butler answering the door to Mr. Death, and he asks, "And who shall I say is calling?" It's rather morbid, but beautiful and simple, mostly acoustic guitar and strings. I listened to it fifty times without getting bored. I have this idea that maybe being at Wallenberg can help me be a poet. It's so lonesome and romantic, and I do believe I'd look fetching in a black turtleneck and French cigarette between my lips.

God, it's funny I was thinking about these things right after Mama died, not about how I was going to pay the rent or take care of myself. I guess I'm not very practical.

◫

September 8.

It's almost three in the morning. Tomorrow's the first day of school. I can't fall asleep. I feel nervous, but a good kind of nervous.

Nick asked me today if I have a gun. I said, "No."

He said, "Alright."

Then he took a small knife from the kitchen drawer, put it in his coat pocket, and left. That was this afternoon. I heard him come in at around one, but I didn't want to get up and see him, in case he was drunk or cut up or God knows what else.

So, he's probably a drug dealer, or maybe a mugger, but still, he actually knows who Leonard Cohen is. We were eating breakfast (he said the eggs I made must have been hatched by diseased chickens) when "Sisters of Mercy" came on the radio. Nick started singing along. I was shocked, not just because he knew the song, but that his voice wasn't so bad. In fact, it was pretty damn good. And I don't know if he's lying or not (I don't really know anything about Nick), but he says he saw Leonard Cohen perform live in Greece eight or nine years ago. Wow!

He also gave me more money, twenty dollars for clothes, not so much, but I managed to buy this cool purple and gold used vest in Kensington Market, along with a black turtleneck and some peace earrings and quite possibly I now look like someone Leonard Cohen would write a song about.

¤

September 9.

A big day. Wallenberg is unbelievably ugly and dirty and it looks like the janitors are on strike (they're not). I guess the filth gives the place ambiance or something.

My homeroom class is my best, Holocaust Studies. I may be grim, but I want to know the depths that man (as in men, not mankind) has sunk to. The teacher's name is Peter Schmidt, and he wants us to call him Peter, which is refreshing, no power trips. He's young and wears jeans, and he admitted he was a "rookie" teacher and we were his first students ever.

The bell rang, and Peter started taking attendance when this beautiful dark-skinned girl walked in. She was wearing a poncho like in the spaghetti westerns, and her long black hair was flowing behind her, she was walking so fast. She took a seat next to me and smiled.

I said, "Here," when Peter called my name, and right after that he called out "Krushalya Samad" (I think that's how it's spelt) and the girl beside me said, "Here." Krushalya Samad. What a great name.

The rest of my classes were okay, except gym, with an insane, whistle-abusing drill sergeant named Mrs. Swan, who, even though more than half the class (including me) didn't bring shorts or running shoes, made us run six laps around the track. Well, we only walked, really, but still. My period came today, too, cramps like a live pig, so that made the experience just a little more hellish than it could have been.

There's no cafeteria at Wallenberg. Anyway, the school's right on Bloor, so there's all this fast food junk. I didn't have much money on me, so I bought some fries from a burger joint and ate them on the school lawn. That's when the girl from Holocaust Studies, Krushalya, walked by with this guy in a U.S. Army jacket (three stripes — is that a captain or a major?). She smiled and said hi, which I guess isn't a big deal to her but it was nice, she's the only person in the whole school whose name I know and I think we'll be friends.

It's not even ten and I feel so tired. Nick's gone. I hope he doesn't wake me up when he comes home.

In general, I'm feeling optimistic. (Lots of ranks today. *Salut!*)

&#9737;

September 10.

My right hand's killing me because Mrs. Swan made us play this barbaric game called dodgeball, the

object of which is to hit people as hard as you can
with a pumped-up volleyball (extra points for inflict-
ing concussions). This truck of a girl, who can palm
the ball, got me in her sights and let it rip. When I
put my arms up to shield my face, the ball bent my
hand all the way back at the wrist. Mrs. Swan blew
her beloved whistle then, not to ask me why my hand
was blue and double its normal size, but to declare
me OUT.

Gym's the only class I hate. The creative writing teacher's name is Joan Tobias, and she's a published poet. She brought in one of her books, titled
*Where the Mice Aren't*. It's a thin paperback with a
mean-looking grey and white cat on the cover. Joan
says we'll workshop one poem or story each period,
and then discuss writing techniques or anything else
we want to talk about. Today we did a poem of hers,
about a lonely old woman who finds her cupboards
overrun with mice. She's disgusted at first, and sets
out traps and poison dust. After a baby mouse
breaks his neck in a trap, the woman feels guilty. She
falls in love with all the mice and lets them take over
her house. My turn to present is Monday, so I have
all weekend to think of something.

At lunchtime, I sat on the school lawn again,
eating my peanut butter sandwich in the cool shade
of a red cedar. Krushalya walked by and began talking to me. She has fabulous hair, long, pitch-black
like some Amazon warrior queen, combed over one
side of her head. Her black eyes breathe, I swear
she's not just seeing with them but hearing and
smelling, touching and tasting. When she caught me
staring, I lowered my gaze to her feet, where I saw
these small runners, I mean really small, it made me
think her beauty's too big for her shoes, which
sounds like a line from a bad country song. I admit

I'm getting carried away, but I've never been fascinat-
ed by anyone before.

She was in the middle of eating a tangerine
when she noticed my Third Reich book on the grass.
"Do you like the class so far?"

I nodded.

"You're new. Most of us Wallenbergers are
either activists or artists. Punks or poets, basically."

"Alright, I confess: I like to write."

She smoothed out a crease in her poncho to
reveal a red button pinned there, a yellow hammer
and sickle on it. "And I like to protest capitalist
swine." The bell rang, and I waited while Krushalya
collected the tangerine peels in her hand. When we
parted in the hallway, she said, "See you tomorrow,
Mara." In some indescribable way, it felt good hearing her say my name.

After school I checked out some bookstores. I
read poems by Stevie Smith, including a neat one I
hadn't seen before, "Not Waving But Drowning." I
love the way she writes, so larky and whimsical on
the surface that you get fooled, and by the end it
dawns on you how bleak and shitty everything is.

Oh, God, I just remembered. Last Sunday a
strange one-armed man, whose front teeth were black
(or maybe even missing, although he was quite young),
asked me on the street if I was sleepwalking. He had a
dirty brown beard and what the olde-tyme poets call
"the look of the dead" in his blue eyes, so I ignored
him, kept on walking, and hoped he'd find someone
else to haunt. But he followed me for an hour, limping,
a tall, frail-looking man who for some reason I couldn't
shake, he was always about ten feet behind me, mutter-
ing, "Lies, lies, lies," over and over again.

I started to feel like I *was* sleepwalking, that it
was all a dream, that everything I see is a painted
mask and something horribly ugly lurks underneath.

I'm going to stop now, I'm crying.  My mother's dead.

⋈

## 12

I kept the journal for a couple of months. I've been sitting here reading it and drinking the blood of Christ, a 1989 vintage from California.

Do you recall, gentle reader, the tale of the Slaughter of the Innocents? Three wise men — Gold, Frankincense, Myrrh — travel many miles to ask King Herod, "Where is he that is born King of the Jews? For we have seen his star in the east, and are come to worship him." Herod orders his soldiers to slay every male child in Bethlehem under the age of two. The soldiers slaughter all the baby boys in Bethlehem. Except baby Jesus.

Say what you want about Him, God looks after His own.

⋈

Most people know nothing about Yugoslavia. Okay, perhaps two things, both related to the city of Sarajevo: the 1984 Winter Olympics, and the 1914 assassination of the archduke Franz Ferdinand (you know, the bullet that launched the First World War). Now, at the bookstore where I work, there's Sarajevo again, on the covers of newspapers and magazines, photographs of broken men and women, murdered, still clenching the loaves of bread they had waited hours in line to buy. The blood in the street, a gaudy red syrup. All of this occurs during a ceasefire, a nice compound word that has absolutely no meaning in Yugoslavia. Above these snapshots of wretchedness, baritone-voiced headlines announce SLAUGHTER IN SARAJEVO. (Amusing, the news media's silly infatuation with alliteration: were the cities changed, it might be MASSACRE IN MOSCOW, or KABOOM IN KABUL.)

I'm going to tell you about that 1914 bullet, fired by one Gavrilo Princip on June 28th. A handsome university student, Gavrilo was a member of *Crna Ruka* (the Black Hand), a gang of angry young men operating within the larger group People's Defense, who belonged to Young Bosnia, who in turn took their cue from the fearsome Union or Death, a national underground movement that sought independence for Slav states from the Austro-Hungarian Empire. Union or Death (a catchy, succinct and self-explanatory moniker) advocated freedom for Slavic peoples by any means necessary, preferably violent. Their symbol — a death's head, dagger, bomb and poison bottle — covered most of the bases. Why Gavrilo would join forces with these rough-talking, chain-smoking men, who believed in God and facial hair but not in bathing or foreplay, is a routinely overlooked question. Until now.

Gavrilo had a big problem. His penis, when fully erect, was over a foot long. This impressed many people in his hometown; unfortunately, all of them were men. No girl wanted Gavrilo. Even Anna Sakić, a kind-hearted prostitute who read musty translations of Dickens by candle-light, refused to service him out of a deep sense of self-preservation. What I am saying is, no one wanted to fuck Gavrilo.

So Gavrilo daily, hourly, dealt with this frustrated heterosexual energy bubbling up inside him.

Soccer was just not release enough. Eventually he purchased a small French pistol and used it to destroy rats and squirrels. He shot branches off trees. He fired at clouds. It helped, but only a little.

Then one day, riding a multi-colored bicycle his father had pieced together from the parts of many old ones, Gavrilo spotted an attractive green and white poster recruiting members for the local chapter of the Black Hand (and what a name!). He promptly dismounted and signed himself up.

Regarding the Archduke Franz Ferdinand, I should mention that he was not all that bad a man. He proposed the creation of a semi-autonomous region of Slavs within the Austro-Hungarian Empire. Not total independence, no, but a more liberal stance than that taken by most of his imperious fellow countrymen.

Timing is crucial. Historians maintain that the date of the archduke's visit to Sarajevo was ill-chosen: June 28th is *Vidovdan*, a national day of mourning for Serbia's defeat at Kosovo Polje in 1389. This loss relegated most Slavic peoples to Turkish rule for five hundred years. Therefore, history books will tell you, the sight of the archduke being driven about town in his limousine on this holy day incited the people of Sarajevo, and specifically Gavrilo, to murder.

Wrong. Timing *is* crucial, that much can't be denied. The sun fell slowly on June 27th, leaving behind a warm, lazy evening. Stars twinkled against the blue-black sky. Crickets chirped. And, from across the lovely dandelion-filled meadow, Gavrilo heard the sound of several men, obviously imbued with spirits, singing to the notes of a badly-played accordion.

Gavrilo, tired of both the Black Hand and his own, had just made love to a slender teen-aged boy named Marko Kolić on the hay and dirt inside an abandoned barn. Lying back, arms folded behind his head, Gavrilo opened, then closed, then opened, then closed his eyes. He was naked and confused. He breathed the air.

In the darkness, to Gavrilo's left, Kolić dressed himself while whistling a nonsense tune. He thought about his mother's tasty beef stew, and whether his husky sisters would leave any for him.

Suddenly Gavrilo, his soft penis swinging like a pendulum between his knees, was on his feet and tweaking Kolić's Adam's apple with all his strength. Kolić's thin arms sputtered helplessly, and into his ear Gavrilo whispered, "If you tell anyone, I will kill you."

Kolić broke free of Gavrilo's grip. He buttoned his pants up and sneered, "You coward! Why don't you face what you are?"

Gavrilo quickly found his trousers on the ground beside him and pulled his belt from the loops. With eyes full of tears, he whipped Kolić savagely about the head and shoulders with the buckle end of his belt. A deep gash soon opened on the bridge of Kolić's nose. When Gavrilo stopped briefly to think about what he was doing, Kolić escaped. Gavrilo dropped back down to the ground, palms covering his throbbing temples.

On June 28th, Gavrilo Princip awoke to a new day. He no longer could look himself in the mirror. He wanted to shed his skin; his tongue was a red devil that only reminded him. When his father called him to breakfast — a hearty porridge cooled with goat's milk — Gavrilo could not meet the old man's eyes.

Along came Archduke Franz Ferdinand, sitting nonchalantly in the back seat of a shiny black limousine with his shiny white wife. It was noon, and the early-morning mist had cleared from the valley in which Sarajevo lies. Gavrilo stood alone at the edge of the gravel road. He loaded his pistol with hands as steady as a sunset. He waited for the limo.

CRACK. The shot missed; the limo sped away unscathed as two shots followed after it. CRACK CRACK. Nothing. Gavrilo was so furious he emptied the pistol into the nearest pear tree. CRACK CRACK CRACK.

Amazingly, the limo crossed a small bridge, circled, and returned. The archduke was determined to visit a friend of his in the hospital, and damn the snipers.

Gavrilo, surprised but grateful for the second chance, reloaded his pistol. He ran alongside the embankment of the bridge and waited for the approaching limo. He raised his pistol. CRACK CRACK CRACK CRACK CRACK CRACK.

The limo stopped. Gavrilo waited. He reloaded once more, just in case, and walked cautiously toward the stalled vehicle. All over. The archduke was dead, head buried ignobly in his own lap. His wife, too, leaning against the door she had attempted futilely to open. The chauffeur, who was of the opinion that the party should not return across the bridge but was too afraid to speak up on the matter, lay slumped and bleeding on the dashboard, dead as the others. Gavrilo threw his pistol into the grey Miljacka River. He smiled, looked up at the sun, and felt his penis harden.

Today, that bridge is called Princip's Bridge. The spot Gavrilo stood and fired six shots is marked by footprints set in concrete. He is a national hero.

If we go back about nine hundred years from Gavrilo's time, we uncover the beginnings of the

excessive violence so prevalent throughout
Yugoslavia's history. In 1014, the Slavs were under
attack from the east by the Byzantine Empire.
Leading the Slavs was a square-jawed young man
named Samuilo, fourth and youngest son of Nicholas
of Macedonia. Samuilo was thrust into the role by
three brothers who feared the Byzantine emperor,
Basil the Second. Samuilo feared him just as much,
but he had no younger brother to whom he could
pass the throne.

Basil the Second's reputation for brutality was
well-deserved. Often he trained the newest soldiers
in his army himself. He enjoyed demonstrating to
the fresh-faced lads the aggressiveness required for
battle. Basil the Second demonstrated on a live goat.
He would lift the unsuspecting animal high in the air
and, with teeth he had shaved down to razor-sharp
points, tear at its hairy throat until blood squirted
forth. The goat's head jerked spastically, and Basil
the Second would drop it to the ground and lick the
blood from his greedy lips. The goat, lying on its side
and unable to move, wasted its dying moments trying to figure mankind.

The two armies met on a warm spring morning. There was no humidity. Samuilo's men outnum-
bered Basil's two-to-one. Ten-to-one wouldn't have
been enough. The Slavs lost resoundingly to their
fiercer opponents, many of whom had emulated their
leader's peculiar but intimidating dental style. Most
of the Slavs, over fourteen thousand of them, were
surrounded on the banks of the Sturma River. Some,
including Samuilo, managed to flee to a nearby village. Little hope was held for the soldiers who were
trapped.

A week later, a sentry reported to Samuilo that
about one hundred men, apparently soldiers who

were stuck on the Sturma, had been sighted making their way to the village. The news was a boost to the low morale of Samuilo's men, who wept openly upon learning that some of their brothers had survived the massacre.

The joy was short-lived. Basil was sending the men back, all fourteen thousand of them, one hundred at a time. Each one of them had had his eyes plucked out with daggers, except for one man, left with one eye to guide the rest back to Samuilo. Accompanied by a grotesque, low-buzzing moan — the sound of a million angry bumblebees — the men descended onto the village like ghosts of themselves, always in groups of one hundred, for six days and nights, all blinded but one. The terrible shock drove Samuilo to drunkenness, then to fever, then to God, then fever again, and, in the end, suicide.

Or consider Dušan, the revered Serbian emperor in the mid-fourteenth century. Dušan detested how time-consuming it was to determine the penalty for each new crime and criminal as they came along, so he founded the first *Zakonik*, or Legal Code. To ensure that the laws were just and humane and in keeping with the word of God, Dušan enlisted the assistance of the Orthodox Church in writing up the code. Thereafter, the penalty for every crime — theft, adultery, murder, what have you — consisted of the cutting off (or pulling out) of one or more of the following body parts: fingers, toes, hands, feet, arms, legs, breasts, buttocks, testicles, tongues, noses, ears and, perhaps with a nod to Basil the Second, eyes. The unofficial record-holder was one Goran Pavelic, a pickpocket with poor hand-to-eye co-ordination who lost both hands, one leg, a testicle, an ear, an eye, his tongue and upper lip. Goran was what is nowadays known as a repeat offender.

There is a saying among Slavic women when the well of luck dries up: "I couldn't escape misery if I married a despot." It comes from Jefimija, a girl who knew misery like carrion knows flies. In appearance, Jefimija was average in every way. She was not exceptionally intelligent. Her personality did not sparkle like icicles in the sunshine. She knew few card tricks and her parents were indentured pig farmers. So, how did a plain-looking peasant girl come to marry a despot?

Jefimija had one special quality — a haunting, sepulchral singing voice. With her mouth open she mesmerized people, made them weep like maudlin drunks, even when she sang the alphabet (which she knew by heart, barely). Her father, upon discovering this gift, volunteered Jefimija for the church choir. She sang every Sunday to an eager congregation.

Word soon reached Despot Ugljes the Unclean, who condescended to attend religious ceremonies for the first time in a dozen years. When his dark, tenebrous eyes met the incongruous image of the skinny, hollow-cheeked girl with the full-bodied wail, he was instantly enchanted. The Unclean waited for the song to end, wiped his tears away and took Jefimija to his castle, pulling her up a hill by a rope tied round her waist while he rode on horseback.

The next day was the wedding day. Jefimija wore a white dress with a red velvet collar. Her family was proud, and her father kissed her cheek and said, "You're a lucky girl."

Two days later the Unclean, having concluded that Jefimija's parents and seven brothers were diverting her attention from him, had his in-laws hanged in a festive ceremony that featured four lute players and eleven Egyptian-trained dancers. Jefimija did not cry out at seeing her entire family dangling from the gallows; she was certain it was all a strange dream. She was ten years old.

Jefimija liked to sing every day outside the castle walls. She sang and watched sparrows and dragonflies gliding over the green moat. At night, she sang in her husband's bed. The Unclean never abused her; he abused himself while she sang. Jefimija found her husband neither appealing nor repulsive, so that when he was slain in the Battle of Marica in 1371, she felt nothing.

After the Unclean's death, Jefimija was allowed to remain with her in-laws, who thought of her as a servant. On the day of her husband's funeral, she was seduced by a doe-eyed stable boy who had loved her from the day his master brought her home. Jefimija became pregnant. Her in-laws believed it to be the despot's heir, and their treatment of her improved greatly.

Jefimija went into labor during a pitiless midnight blizzard. The baby was born with three growths on its tiny forehead, the shape and color of walnuts. The growths, which were moist, gave the convincing and horrifying illusion that they were breathing. The baby's toes were webbed, as well, and its lips were joined so that the mouth could not be opened. The attendant midwife, upon recovering from her second fainting spell, was beaten to death on the spot and later buried in a shallow grave behind the stable. The baby was suffocated. Jefimija never saw her daughter's face.

In 1389 came the infamous loss at Kosovo Polje. Jefimija, a figure of the ruling class, was publicly raped by the Turkish soldiers. After they tired of her and unchained her, Jefimija walked and walked, winding up in Serbia. She found refuge in Prince Lazar's court.

The prince was a generous man. He listened to Jefimija's story and felt a sincere sympathy for her. He invited her to live with him and he came to love her deeply, spending much of his free time teaching her to read and write. But in a year he was dead, killed by the Turks.

And Jefimija finally wept.

A convent gave her shelter, and in time she became a nun. After a vow of silence that lasted twenty years, she requested a sewing needle, some silk and plenty of fine gold thread. For the rest of her life, Jefimija embroidered the eulogies of those she had lost into a giant silk quilt. When she died, no one at the convent knew she could sing.

⋈

What follows is the final paragraph of the first book I ever read about my ancestral homeland:

*We hope the outline which we have given of the Yugoslav people will help our many English-speaking readers to understand some of the differences between our way of life and theirs. Their experience has been different from our own; because of it, their ways of thought have been cast in a different mould. Underlying these differences, however, is our common humanity. Every year, more and more visitors from the West are discovering the very beautiful land of Yugoslavia, and they are finding that they are received with warm hospitality and friendship. We would like to think that the foregoing pages will make some contribution to the furtherance of this special friendship. And, most happily, there is no doubt that the worst excesses of the struggle between the nationalists which once warped the development of Yugoslavia are now only a bitter memory of the past.*

Published in 1961, this exquisitely-bound book was imaginatively, if immodestly, titled *Yugoslavia,* and printed in Great Britain as part of a "Nations of the Modern World" series by a press that actually called itself Books That Matter.

As an impressionable young girl wielding her library card — "A passport to knowledge," Miss Henderson soberly informed us — I dare say I used to look forward to that royal "we" found in so many British books about Yugoslavians and other "others." Share a common humanity with the English? Jolly good. And how about the charitable predictions for those warm, friendly and different Yugoslavs? Silly excesses? Pah! Thing of the past.

⋈

I'm thinking about Gavrilo again, how the assassination of the archduke was so unusual in that he was a foreigner and the preferred targets for Slavs are other Slavs. Like Scepan Mali, a one-eyebrowed scamp who came to power in Montenegro by telling everyone he had made love to Catherine the Second of Russia (yeah sure, Scepan); he wound up sucking sword in 1774.

In 1860, Prince Danilo of Montenegro was strangled with his own pants.

In 1861, they found Prince Michael of Serbia face down in a puddle of blood; diamond rings adorned his little-lady fingers, but his heart and liver were gone.

Alexander Obrenović ruled Serbia for a while, until he made the mistake of marrying one Draga Mašin, an early European feminist. Thin-lipped Draga would hike up her long black skirt, climb the creaking soap-box and caterwaul away on universal suffrage and other assorted women's issues. Grated on the nerves, etc. So, on Christmas Day, 1903, ten brave army officials took Lizzie Borden's axe and administered forty whacks on Alex; Draga took forty-one.

My God, they must be genetically pro-grammed. Different. If this is how they treated their leaders, then I don't even want to dream about how they treated each other, especially during World War Two. Especially during now.

Now. I'll finish this bottle of wine and go to bed. Tomorrow, I'm off to Pearson airport for the early-evening flight to Belgrade. I'm going to meet my brother again.

⋈

# 13

September 14.

It's been a few days. Everything just got to me all at once. The tears began gushing that evening and didn't stop until the sun came up. Nick came in from wherever he goes at night. He knocked on my door and left a bottle of red wine for me in the hallway. I swigged it from the jug like an alley drunk, crying and drinking all night until I passed out.

When I woke up, my head felt like a flushing toilet. It was two-thirty in the afternoon; school was a missed train. So, food. And while making myself a sandwich, I noticed the t.v. was gone. Nick was sprawled on the couch, right in front of where it used to be, reading the paper, scratching his parts. I bit into my grilled cheese and asked, "Where's the t.v.?"

He looked convicted: "You never watched it! It's bad for you, it makes you blind and sterile. Be quiet, I'm reading the sex crimes."

"So, where is it?"

"I traded it for a guitar," he said, more irritated than guilty.

I took another bite. "So, where's the guitar, then?"

"At... my... girlfriend's... house," he said, growling.

"What girlfriend?"

He lowered the paper and glared at me. "No one likes a nosy alcoholic."

"Thanks for the wine."

I made him move his feet and I sat down beside him.

"Is it an acoustic?"

"Yeah. You don't play, do you?"

"No. I'd like to learn though."

He smirked. Then he went back to reading his rag. And that's the whole story — my first drinking binge and hangover. Pretty lame. No sex-orgy antics or pissing in public fountains.

The next day, Friday, I didn't get off the subway at Spadina to go to school. I felt too depressed, all those morning faces. I stayed on until Yonge, got off, went to the library and read poems for a few hours, even ones by Ted Hughes.

So here it is, late Sunday night. I wasted the weekend lying in bed and moping like a kicked dog. To top it off, the poem I've been working on for my writing class is — thank you, Mr. Roget — excrementy.

¤

September 15.

I almost threw up today in Holocaust Studies. I wasn't the only one upset — someone left the room, there was sniffling, too. Peter showed us a documentary, black and white with no sound, about a concentration camp in Poland: the Allied Forces had defeated Germany and were freeing survivors. It was sickening, seeing it up close on a screen, the faces of children, the snakepits full of spindly bodies twisted into one another. One little boy, he was pale milky skin stretched over bones, he was so weak that two stronger boys had to prop him up. After an American soldier lifted him onto the back of a truck, I stopped watching. It ruined my whole day. What I mean is, I couldn't get all those faces out of my mind, especially the boy's. He was only about ten years old.

Krushalya invited me to Fatso's for lunch. Five kids from class were there, and none of us felt like talking. Or eating. The waitress came over, and we ordered only three soft drinks, which made her kind of mad, she put her hand on her hip. It *was* the window table, after all.

Krushalya asked, quite unexpectedly, "Where were you last week?"

"Measles," I blurted out. I'm lousy under pressure.

"Quick recovery."

We didn't say much after that. She knows I lied, but I hope she doesn't take it personally.

When I got home, it was surprise time. From Nick's room — my parents' room — I heard a woman making sexual ecstasy-type noises. I was doing math homework in the kitchen; Nick's girlfriend walked in, naked and proud. "Hi," she chirped, all smiles. "My name's Karen."

"Hi," I said, my eyes glued to problem 5a.

"Kind of chilly out here, don't you think?" She took some orange juice from the fridge, filled up two glasses, and made small talk with me — what grade I'm in, what are my hobbies, blah, blah, blah. I mean, she was naked! Two tits, a bush and butt cheeks! "Chilly!" I wanted to shout. "You idiot, you're standing nude in front of a stranger with your nipples hard!" Finally she said, "Sorry to bother you, see you later." I saw bitemarks on her bum.

I need a friend. Or else I'll start lighting fires in my wastebasket again.

✕

September 16.

Karen was up before anyone, wearing only Nick's t-shirt (I wonder if she came over here without any clothes at all). She made coffee and French toast for breakfast. It creeped me a bit, like she was pretending to be my mom sending me off to school. But it smelled good, so I sat with her and ate.

Her bouncing brown hair and brilliant white teeth make her look perky, like a t.v. weather girl: "Mister Sun will rise at six-oh-seven tomorrow morning and set at five-thirty."

There I was, smothering my French toast in grape jelly, when out of the blue Karen said, "Nick tells me you're interested in guitars."

"Yeah," I said, stopping the bread an inch from my mouth.

"I play a little. If you want, I could give you lessons."

It seemed fishy. "I don't know," I said.

She gulped some coffee and added, "Free."

"Okay," I said. "Thanks."

"Can you read music at all?"

"I played the recorder in grade school. I've forgotten it all, though."

"No problem, you'll pick it up. Come to my place Friday after school?"

"Sure."

She wrote her address down and went back to Nick's room.

School was better. No dodgeball in gym, someone let the air out of the volleyballs (wish I'd thought of that). We just ran laps for forty minutes. I hate long distance running, all that useless, numbing effort, but it beats getting balls whipped at your head from three directions.

In Holocaust Studies, we discussed yesterday's film (Krushalya wasn't there, and it felt sort of weird sitting alone at our desk). Peter brought in a stack of books, personal accounts of the holocaust, and told us to choose one with the idea of writing an essay. *The Diary of Anne Frank* was there, but I've read it. I picked *Babi Yar*. I thought "babi" might mean "baba" — grandmother in Yugoslavian — but it's the name of a Ukrainian town where a lot of Jews were killed.

◫

September 17.

Just got back from High Park with Krushalya, where we hung out pretty late after seeing *A Clockwork Orange* at The Bloor Cinema. After the movie we bought two cups of tea and walked all the way to the park. As soon as we got there, a mother raccoon, with three little ones following in a line, passed in front of us. They look spooky at night, all hunched over with crazy grins, like Doctor Jekyll cats after drinking the potion. We found a nice hidden place to sit, just beyond the park's winding road. The grass felt cool and wet. Krushalya undid the buttons of her green army jacket and crossed her legs. "Are you sure it's not too late for you?" she asked. "Won't your parents mind?"

I had decided not to lie to her about anything. I want a friend I can be honest with. "My mother's dead, and I don't know where my father is."

"You live alone?"

"With my uncle."

She lifted the tea bag out of her cup and clipped the lid back on. And she changed the subject right away. "My parents are in Guyana," she said.

"Really? Is that in Asia?"

"South America. A tiny country north of Brazil. We moved here when I was a baby, and then, two years ago, my parents wanted to go back."

"And you stayed here?"

She folded her legs underneath herself now (she never settles on one position). "My father announced one day that we were going to Guyana for the summer. It sounded great to me. Except that my father intended to live there forever, a fact he didn't share with anyone else."

"Why did he want to live there?"

"He got fed up with Canada. He could never get a better job than cab driver. Plus, he said Toronto was turning me into a slut." She laughed when she saw my reaction: "You don't have to blush, you know."

"No, I think it was the tea, it's too hot," I stammered. I'm such a virgin.

"You're funny, Mara." She unfolded her legs and suddenly got serious. "Do you mind if I ask you about your mom?"

"No. Not really. No."

Her voice softened. "When did she die?"

"The middle of August."

"Was she sick?"

"Sort of," I said, with a lump in my throat.

We drank our tea and didn't talk for a while. In the distance, bicycle tires made sizzling noises on the night road. I wanted to say something. I didn't want her to think I was having traumatic childhood flashbacks or anything. So I asked, "How did you get out of Guyana?"

"Where to begin.  First, I was only fourteen then, and I went nuts when I realized what'd happened.  Getting kidnapped is very unpleasant.  It really sucks.  For about a week, I was swearing, throwing tantrums, and my father, who's more religious than God, was swearing and hitting me."

"He was hitting you?"

"Oh yeah, he's not squeamish about that at all.  He has this windmill move, both arms whirling around and around, slapping my poor head about a thousand times a second."  She illustrated briefly, her arms scissoring the air in front of her.  "After a few days of that, we both got tired."

I was shocked.

"I wrote my friends in Toronto.  They started a collection and sent me a money order for a plane ticket back.  The day I got it, I put on a Muslim dress that covered everything but my eyeballs.  I told my parents I'd been wicked, and that I wanted to go to the mosque and pray."

"They believed you?"

She gave me a wry little smile.  "Sure.  Outsmarting your parents is what evolution is all about."

"Darwin didn't say that."

"I inferred it."

I laughed.

"Only I'd forgotten to call ahead for flight information.  I'd hitch-hiked forty miles to Georgetown and there I was, all dusty and anxious to fly, and it turned out there wasn't a plane going to Toronto for two days."

"What did you do?"

"I slept on a bench at the airport.  The security guards gave me a hard time.  One of them tried to steal my backpack, I was actually wrestling with this skinny goon while his pals watched. Another one kept coming on to me, trying to get me to go into the washroom with him. When I said I was fourteen, he said, 'So am I, baby.' He had a wedding ring."

"Gross."

"It's interesting with men: normally they're pigs, but put any kind of uniform on them and they become pigs with fangs."

"And that's where you stayed for two days and nights?"

"Yeah. I expected my father, or maybe even the police, to storm down that grey corridor and drag me away. But no one came for me. And when my plane finally took off, I was on it. My mother wrote me a letter, all tear-stained, saying when my father discovered all my stuff was gone he just said, 'Forget it.' My mother still writes, asking me to forgive my father and come back."

She stopped there, and I was going to ask her if she misses her mother, but that would have been a stupid question.

I was in a good mood when I got home, and it got even better when Nick opened the door for me while I was looking for my keys. He closed the door behind me and fastened the chain lock. "Where have you been?"

I had some fun with the old boy. "Were you worried?" I grinned.

"No." He scratched his head and turned away. "And why are you smiling like that? You look like the village idiot we used to chase."

I think he was worried. What a great day.

⋈

September 20.

Ooh, I'm a sucker. It was sunny outside, and I stayed home and cried reading *Babi Yar*. I broke down when I got to the story of Dina Pronicheva:

After watching Jews, including her own parents, being shot and dumped into a huge pit the Nazis had dug up, Dina herself was lined up to be executed. She leapt into the pit before the machine guns reached her.

The soldiers hopped into the pit and shot anyone still moving. Dina, despite being kicked in the breast, gave no signs of life. However, when sand was shovelled into the giant grave, Dina decided that a bullet was better than being buried alive — she moved a little for air, and no one noticed.

When darkness came, Dina crawled over the dead bodies with Motya, a young boy who'd also survived. They slept in the daytime and walked at night. Motya would run ahead and act as a look-out, shaking a bush if no Nazis were around. One time there were, and Dina looked on in silence as they shot Motya.

Eventually Dina escaped the most dangerous zone, only to be ratted on by her fellow Ukrainians. She was again loaded onto a truck heading for Babi Yar. Only Dina wasn't returning to that nightmare no matter what. She took a chance and jumped from the back of the truck. Freedom.

Even though she's still alive and working in a puppet theatre, it feels like she died.

¤

September 21.

I just got back from peeing. Nick was in the living room, choking his guitar (the only way I can describe that noise) and singing in Serbian about a sexy gypsy lady with no shoes. He stopped me with his, "Hey, kid." The asshole's forgotten my name, if he ever knew it. He lay on the floor, flat on his back. He asked if I'd ever been to "Beograd" (he's told me before not to call it "Belgrade"). When I said I hadn't, he replied, "Everyone goes there sometime."

¤

September 25.

This is the poem I brought in today:

*The Snake's Face*

*A snake is a thing*
*you cannot predict. When kissing*

*the pig's cheek he will not*
*smile or threaten or break down*

*into sobs of confession. A snake*
*is an engine that hisses all night.*

The comments from the class were positive for the most part, although some people thought the meaning was unclear. Can't argue there. I wrote it a few nights ago after an especially twisted nightmare: I saw my parents walking in the Garden of Eden. When I called out to them, they turned around, and I saw that they had no eyes. They couldn't see me, of course, and they didn't recognize my voice, and, well, I had too nice a day, forget that depressing shit.

Krushalya, Dave, Ling Ling and I took off at lunch today for Lake Ontario. Dave is in my writing and holocaust classes. He's got friendly green eyes, light brown hair (wavy, never combed), and he's tall and thin. Sort of off-beat cute. He has a funny walk, like a hiccup, he takes a few strides, then his left leg kicks out, straightens itself and repeats the whole process. I'm no chiropractor, but I'd say it's a knee thing. Ling Ling's also in the holocaust class. She's a cool girl, very pretty, always cracking jokes about the goofy guys who ask her out. Her parents own a clothing store on Dundas, so she's always wearing neat new skirts and sweaters, usually in red and white, her two favorite colors.

Dave wanted to take the Bathurst bus down to the lake, but I suggested Islington and then the street-car across. I wanted to bring them to the shore near my apartment, because most people never see it, and it's a shame, it's so peaceful. The ride dragged on a bit and Dave and Ling Ling complained, but when we got there all three of them were surprised by how gorgeous it was, the grey-blue water reflecting the sun and warm wind blowing softly over us. A few ducks squawked for crumbs, as did the McDonald's birds, who prefer fries. We sat four across on three rocks, Krushalya and me on the middle one, Ling Ling beside her and Dave beside me. It was so quiet, our backs turned to the world, watching the waves roll in and Buffalo so far away we couldn't see the buildings burning. Dave, who has a flair for strange questions — once he asked Joan, "Would a poet who types with his nose have a better chance of being original?" — asked us about the saddest day of our lives.

"You're a fun guy, Dave," Krushalya said.

"Sadness is poetic," he said. "It's spiritual, and educational. You don't learn anything winning the lottery. What about you, Ling Ling?"

"Me? My saddest day? I'm afraid I'll have to disqualify myself."

"Why?"

"Because," she said, tossing her head back like a cover girl ready for her close-up, "I'm sixteen and beautiful and the saddest days are yet to come."

"Like next Wednesday?" Krushalya asked.

Ling Ling giggled and threw tiny black stones in the lake. "Don't bug me about that again."

"What's next Wednesday?" I asked.

"Ling Ling's getting her eyes done."

"What do you mean?"

"You may have noticed, Mara," Krushalya said, "that Ling Ling happens to be Chinese. She wants to change that."

"Come on," Ling Ling said, not giggling anymore.

Krushalya shook her head and sighed.

"They're just my eyelids. I'm not transplanting my head. It's just two eyelids. One. Two."

"Fine," Krushalya said, with an ever louder sigh.

"They're my fucking eyes, so stop making that face at me!"

A quiet moment. Then Dave whistled a couple of notes and said, "Are we finished with the eyelids, then?"

"Thank you," Ling Ling said.

"Now, back to what we were talking about. If —"

Krushalya interrupted: "You mean what *you* were talking about."

"I stand corrected. Boy, you're difficult today."

"I'm not on the rag, if that's what you're getting at."

Dave putt-putted his lips. "God, no! Sometimes you've got no culture at all, Krushalya. Anyway, what was *your* saddest day?"

"Monday. When Ling Ling told me about the operation."

We all groaned.

"Alright, I give up. You're so into this sadness thing, you talk, Dave."

"Well, if you really want me to."

"That's not what I said," Krushalya laughed. "But go on, sad boy."

Dave went on. "Three summers ago, my dad and I went up to our cabin by Lake Killarney. We brought our dog, Vengeance."

"Nice name," Ling Ling said.

"Thank you. Vengeance was a terrific beagle we'd had for six years, since he was a puppy. He was very protective. When I was eight or nine, this bully would frequently beat the crap out of me — usually, but not exclusively, in a park near my house. Once, Vengeance followed me without my knowing, and when the guy started fitting his knuckles in my ear, Vengeance jumped him. He knocked the guy to the ground and tore a bloody chunk out of his calf. What choreography! And, best of all, I never got beat up again."

"That *is* sad," Krushalya said.

"Very droll. Anyway, we had a great time up there. It was Vengeance's first trip to the woods. He chased chipmunks and barked at loons and got kicked in the head by a moose he was harassing. He loved it."

Dave rubbed his eyes, and it began to dawn on us that maybe this was a sad story after all.

"The last day, my dad and I woke up and we couldn't find him anywhere. We searched the whole area, yelling 'Vengeance!' over and over again, so hard our lungs ached. The other campers thought we were some runaway religious freaks. We stayed an extra night, but we had to leave the next morning without him. My dad couldn't miss more than one day of work."

"So you lost your dog?"

"I'm not finished. On two different weekends that summer, I hitch-hiked north to look for him. The first time I went with my friend, Chris. We must have walked about a hundred miles looking for Vengeance."

"You find him?"

"No. But Labor Day weekend, I went up alone. I found him. He'd been on his own in the wilderness for seven weeks. He was thinner, his coat was scruffy, but it was him. He was totally fucking wild. Vicious. He bared his teeth at me and growled. Thought I was food. I tried talking to him, I even brought his favorite tennis ball, but he didn't care. Didn't recognize me one bit. For two days I tried to calm him down, but it was no use. I had to leave him there."

"Wow, that's pretty sad," Ling Ling said.

"A few months later, in December during the Christmas break, I dreamt that Vengeance was scratching at our front door. It seemed so real, I swear I heard it. It was incredible. I ran to the door."

"Well," Krushalya said, actually sounding interested, "was it Vengeance?"

"Are you nuts? You think a dog's gonna walk six hundred miles in the dead of winter and find one little house in downtown Toronto?"

"Dave," Krushalya said, "does this story have a point?"

"The point, dear Krushalya, is that the dream was a message. I had to go back to Lake Killarney and find Vengeance. I hitch-hiked again, by myself."

"In December?" I asked.

"I made good time, because the drivers on Highway Eleven felt so sorry for me, rubbing my thighs like I was ready to drop from exposure, puffing cold air just as their cars were approaching. I hammed it up."

He paused, to make sure we appreciated his cunning.

"When I got there, it must have been minus twenty. I walked along the shore of the lake for an hour. I almost tripped over Vengeance; he was dead. Frozen. Lying on his side with his eyes open, and they were not the hateful eyes of the beast I saw on Labor Day, but the loving eyes of my faithful friend. My boy. He looked so tortured and abandoned, an orphan lost in the woods."

Everyone was silent.

"I wanted to bury him. I really did. But I had no shovel, and the ground was harder than cement. So I collected some branches and twigs and built a fire. I peeled off a t-shirt and wrapped Vengeance up in it. I lowered him into the flames. I was in a trance by then, staring at the fire and remembering the good times we'd had, like when he maimed that bully for me."

A seagull splattered a rock with white paste, and we laughed, grateful for the relief.

"I had the fire going strong when, suddenly, there's a family standing next to me, a father, mother and three little brats cross-country skiing, singing 'Alouette' in about six different keys. The father slapped me hard on the back and said, 'Hey, a bonfire! Great idea, son! Mind if we join you?' I must have nodded, because they gathered round Vengeance and pulled their mittens off. Ten hands — fifty fingers, assuming no deformities — warming themselves off my dog!" He shook his head and threw a stone into the water. "And then something *really* gross. Fur and bones started popping up through the branches and t-shirt, and I was terrified that this family, this walking gum commercial, would see this and think I was some psychotic dog killer and barbecuer. So I quietly backed away from them, picked up my knapsack, and took off. I left them there with my poor dog."

No one said anything. I didn't want to look at Dave, I was sure he had tears in his eyes. We watched a steamliner float by.

I really wanted to kiss him by the lake today.

⋈

# 14

The first thing I see after I slam the door shut is the sign affixed to the dashboard. It's a sign found in taxis in cities all over the United States and Canada: a cigarette enclosed in a red circle, with a red line slashing diagonally across the smoking white stick. The cab, gentle reader, smells like a Cabbagetown pool hall at midnight. Not good for my hangover.

"Hello, my friend." He says it *frent*. "What is your destination request?"

How formal. "The airport, please."

"A trip." *A treep.* "That is exciting. Better than chewing your toenails, to be sure. Terminal two, am I to assume?"

"Yes."

He's wearing a navy blue baseball cap, tipped at a rakish angle. I glance at the i.d. photo clipped in the corner of the inch-thick plastic, bullet-proof partition; immediately, I wish I hadn't. A cubist face if ever I saw one, with sinister upside-down eyebrows, and a crazy left eye that droops lower than the right, close to the bottom of the nose, the proboscis of a really bad boxer, a long, mangled, beat-up nose that's praying for the bell.

Then the name catches my eye. Branko Hrvatin. I have two one-word mottos by which I live my life: civility, privacy. I don't pry, and I say thank you and excuse me and I'm sorry so fast my lips don't move. If I happen to be asked a question I deem too personal, I nod in silence, or look away, or mumble to myself, waiting for the awkward moment to die of negligence. But today, for some reason, I cannot be me. "I noticed your name," I say.

A big smile in the rearview mirror, a gold tooth gone dull. He flicks his cigarette at the rolled-up window; the ashes flake down the inside of the cab. "You were trying to determine, my friend, if I may extrapolate such a thing, how to pronounce my last name. The missing vowel, correct?"

"No." How to ask this. "It's a Croatian name, isn't it?"

His smile digs itself a ditch.

"My parents were from Yugoslavia," I say, with no idea where I want this bit of Hello-I'm-over-here to take me.

He sounds suspicious: "Vivisection hurts." His foot presses hard on the gas. "You're not Croatian."

"My mother was from Macedonia."

"Macedonia. A blind man trapped in an out-house during a thunderstorm. The view is divine. Beautiful moon. What about your father?"

"Slovenia," I lie.

"Ljubljana?"

"Yes."

The smile makes a comeback. "The Slovenians have the best *slivovitz* anywhere. Not surprisingly, however, a steady diet of plum brandy and sausages makes them perhaps the world's unhealthiest people, at least among those with access to foodstuffs. Have you ever seen the liver of a Slovenian?"

"No." I've lost control of this, I'm not driving anything.

He pulls his visor down against the last gasp of sun shooting through the darkening clouds. "The situation, my friend: I came to this country twenty years ago. On a tilting Italian ship infested with skinny Yugoslav rats. The Sicilian crew was a carnival of grotesques, not a non-rapist among them. The food was edible, but not digestible. The original source for the meat was anybody's guess. We hung our dicks over the hull of the ship and pissed into the ocean like schoolboys. Even with this inauspicious beginning, leaving my homeland turned out to be the smartest thing I ever did."

He turns the car radio on, spins the tuner without looking, and lands on something with harpsichords, maybe Bach. I want to forget everything: where I'm from, where I am, where I'm going. I close my tired eyes and escape into sleepy ruminations. Any ordinary fantasy will do. Me on a tiny tropical island not found on any map, awakened at dawn by a slow-rising, humming sun. I'm stretched out on a hammock, with pretty young boys fanning me and feeding me cool, fat grapes. I would be their queen, and I'd be benevolent, I would break up their little quarrels before they grew serious, and I would kiss their angelic knees, whether they were scraped or not. We would bathe nude in the still, clear lagoon, the water would refresh us, and daring goldfish would nibble on our calves. We'd swim and splash, and afterwards we'd dry off in the sunshine and eat berries and coconuts and...

"Let me tell you, Yugoslavia was bad, but not like this. Tito was still alive, or at least his twin was, for the first Tito lacked certain digits where the second did not." He shows me the back of his right hand, five bulky fingers spread out, pointing to heaven. Then, slowly, purposefully, he bends the middle and ring fingers out of sight, leaving the horns of a bull. "See? An impostor," he concludes. "Everyone,

including me, believed the second Tito was a lousy
dictator. And his generals were Satan's minions, you
could tell by their excessive dandruff and diabolic
fondness for cats. But what could there be besides a
beast like Josip Broz?"

I'll shut up, it's a rhetorical question. It is.
Stop. A red light. I will look over there, yes, that's
what I'll do, in the park where two dogs of indetermi-
nate breed are — as a Victorian novelist might put it
— recreating themselves.

But in the rearview mirror, a pair of unmatched
brown eyes stare back at me, waiting. I rub my chin
and glance to the side, but too late, he saw me.

"Excuse me, my friend," he says, respectfully.
He just won't let me go. "I said, 'What else could
there be?'"

I don't want to be here. "I don't know."

"I do!" He raps his knuckles three times on
top of the dashboard. "A hammer-fisted, son-of-a-
bitch dictator is the *only* kind of leader for a race of
bedwetters." He breathes in smoke and exhales a
quick burst of laughter. "Sometimes I get sick, it's
true. Sometimes I go away from my mind, way up
there somewhere, on another planet, another ferris
wheel. And sometimes I slip into a big barrel of
drink and lose myself. Don't worry, not when I'm
driving. If you buckle up your seatbelt now, I will be
offended beyond repair."

I slide my hand away from the seatbelt. How
did he see that?

"We're a sick bunch. No foresight, just back-
sight. We live in the past. We eat the past. We want
to take what's already burnt and cook it differently.
Always the past, never the future. Who killed whom,
who is to blame for what. Revenge, revenge, revenge,
and then, when that's done, a *little more* revenge.

Insatiable, bloodsucking leeches with opposable thumbs! Oh, forgive me, my patient friend, as I am susceptible to my own demented harangues. I used to be a literary critic. I wrote for an influential journal called — but you would not have heard of it, never mind. Do you know George Orwell, the writer?"

"Yes." Coffee, I think: he's had ten thousand cups today, black.

"Mister Orwell was a decent man. He said that a nationalist not only does not disapprove of atrocities committed by his own side, but he has a remarkable capacity for not even hearing about them. Yes. I'm Croatian, I know. The Serbs are killers, so are we. Look it up. We did it better fifty years ago. Severed heads on parade. A fine, lusty tradition, began perhaps by that Biblical bitch, Salome, who won John the Baptist's head for shaking her fat boobs at King Herod. Correct. No one from my family speaks to me anymore. A big mouth is what I have beneath my mashed potato of a nose. I saw you looking at my picture. Never mind. My brother calls me a pig and a traitor. He thanks his God that our dear mother is dead and cannot see me now. Such a sentiment would hurt, if I respected the cross-eyed bastard."

He snaps open the glove compartment and pulls out a folded copy of *Danas* (Today). He holds the newspaper up shakily in front of the partition while driving, his eyes turned to me for the first time, his lips curled up in an almost-comical expression of righteous contempt. The entire front page of the newspaper is an extreme close-up of a weeping, wrinkled babushka, with tears thick as mercury flowing down into the trenches of her cheeks.

"Lies!" he bellows, spanking the empty seat beside him with the woman's face. "Do you know what lies are?"

✕

The next ninety minutes blur into airport esca-
lators, passports and muddled daydreams. I'm a girl
again, four, maybe five, sitting up in bed in the old
apartment. It's dark, quiet as a cat's paw. I'm alone
in the apartment, everyone's withered away. The
black telephone in the living room starts to ring. I'm
terrified, but I must answer the phone. I climb out of
bed, and the doorknob isn't where it should be. In
the cold shadows I fumble for it, around and around
the entire room, but no doorknob. The ringing grows
fainter and I begin to panic, to cry, I'm rushing along
the walls, dizzy now, desperate for a way out, but
there is none.

I take my seat on the plane, a window seat
with an unobstructed view of the Virgin Mary bend-
ing over and, no, no, I'm very tired, it's a mechanic in
blue overalls checking the metal flaps on the wing.

The passengers begin to make small talk.
Someone says sanctions will soon forbid air travel to
Serbia. Someone else wonders out loud if her sister
in Dubrovnik is alright; she hasn't heard from "Lepa"
in five weeks. Sarajevo is crumbling, a man says.
Facts, neutral facts, plainly spoken and nonflamma-
ble. How carefully innocuous. I want to stand up on
my seat and shout, "I hear the Serbs have trained
police dogs to rape Croatian babies," or, "Did you
hear about the Muslim kindergarten class the Croats
butchered and then tried to pin on the Serbs?" That
would be funny.

"Please fasten your seatbelt, Miss."

I shut my eyes, breathe evenly and try to
think of a hundred dead martyrs. They have to be
in alphabetical order. If I think of Alfred Dreyfus

after I've already come up with, say, Gandhi, then I can't count him (Dreyfus, that is). And if I'm having trouble — either falling asleep or coming up with the martyrs — then I'll start to cheat and count people who aren't really martyrs but perhaps only misunderstood criminals, like, say, Rasputin, whom I often turn to because R is the eighteenth letter (useful, if I'm still observing my alphabet rule) and because I like to think of the ridiculous way in which he was murdered — poisoned with cyanide-laced cake, shot point-blank in the chest, punted in the head, stabbed in the groin and, finally, drowned, a veritable marathon of pain. I can't believe how long it took his inept enemies to kill him, what a disgrace. And then the nutty legend spread that his huge veiny penis was cut off and kept in a jar by a wart-covered peasant woman who would, in time, pass the pickled prize down through her family, generation to generation, and what do you *do* with a preserved penis, however big and famous, except look at it, I guess.

I'm so tired.

I unbuckle my seatbelt and walk down the beige-carpeted aisle. Every seat I pass is unoccupied. No evidence exists of any passenger: no blankets, no magazines, not a single miniature bottle of complimentary cognac or vodka. I don't stop until I get to the pilot's cabin. I knock on the door.

"Come in."

A dozen plants, heather, I think, line the top of the control panel, the bell-shaped pedals a striking purple against the black clouds that crash the cockpit window. A man sits in one of the chairs, facing straight ahead, and without turning motions for me to take the seat beside him.

He sighs. "I feel a deep, sincere pain reading your letters, as if I were looking at the grief of a girl abandoned by everyone and forgotten. My life is also full of bitterness and gall. My wreath has more thorns than others."

He squeezes my hand with his bony fingers.

"Why are you telling lies about me, Mara?"

I'm fearful and, somehow, ashamed. "Who are you?"

"I'm the assassin."

"Gavrilo?"

Out of the corner of my eye I see him nod.

So this is the end. "Is this hell?"

"No." His laughter is gentle and benign, not at all mocking.

"Where am I?"

"I want to tell you about myself. No one... " He stops himself. "Did you know that I ended up in prison?"

"No."

"An Austrian prison. Theresienstadt. A mean little town where dreams go to die. They kept me chained to a grey wall in a darkened cell. The guards pitied me, yes, but they were ordered, under the severest penalty, not to speak a word to to me. I was lonely. For a while I had a friend, a fellow inmate. He was a kind Jewish doctor who gave me all the candy his fiancée smuggled in to him. We talked through the walls when we could, sometimes for hours at a time, about life and death, poetry and women. He was a brother to me, I loved him. I was crushed when he killed himself."

A quiet moment.

"It was for the best. His life was agony. His fiancée died, I don't know of what, a broken heart. It was too much, for both of them. Doctor Levin was just beginning a twenty-year sentence for giving falsified health certificates to men wanting to avoid military service. He turned no one away, absolutely no one. I myself asked him a great favor, to amputate my left arm, and he did a good job, despite poor conditions and a lack of proper surgical tools."

I finally look at him. A thin face, shaggy brown hair and a patchy growth of beard. A high, strong forehead. And his eyes, light-blue eyes, beautiful, sensitive, intelligent.

"The rest of me, too."

I close my eyes, and then I look. His body is long and frail, a buttoned white undershirt clinging to his caved-in chest, the left arm cut off at the elbow, the legs two lifeless twigs.

"I had no one to talk to for the final two years of my life. The Austrians," he says, with apparent reticence, "would not allow me any letters. I'm sure, *I am sure*, that people wrote to me. Somebody must have. I had many friends."

His head swings from side-to-side.

"I couldn't walk," he begins again. "Tuberculosis. On the very day I was imprisoned, ulcers as big as hands appeared on my belly, full of thick pus." He opens his right hand and gazes meditatively into his palm. He looks at me with a sad grin. "Yes, I winced as well. Actually, it was the first time I wept, seeing those abominations on me."

"I'm sorry," I say, the words puny and useless.

"The disease spread rapidly through my body," he says. "The war had started. I was the enemy, and my treatment wasn't a priority for my captors. They did transfer me to a hospital for my last few days, though. They gave me room number thirteen, the scoundrels." He laughs. "They were only men. I should forgive them."

"What happened in the hospital?"

"Nothing," he says. "The war was winding down. People had lost their families, their homes. It was an accepted truth by then, especially in Austria, that I was the catalyst for all the death and destruction. The doctors at the hospital were not exactly obsessed with saving my miserable life. And so, not without warning, one fine spring day in April of 1918, I died."

He stops and seeks my eyes out; I turn away.

"They planted me in a pleasant enough Catholic cemetery, green grass and yellow butterflies, that sort of thing, but it wasn't what I wanted. Luckily for me, they exhumed my coffin two years later and sent me to Sarajevo, where I got a decent burial in my homeland."

I can feel his blood coursing through my veins.

"Those are the facts," he says, "the neutral facts. I'm a glorious footnote, am I not? The history books identify me as 'a radical Bosnian Serb terrorist,' or some such thing. But that's not me, that's not my life. I could talk about my life, if that would help you. Or we can talk about you, Mara."

"About me? No, I don't want that."

"Very well. The beginning, then. I was born in the summer of 1894, a cloudy day, they say. My mother was milking a cow when she felt me coming up for air. She ran back to the house, kicking all of the cats sleeping in her path, and she threw herself on the earth floor by the open hearth and screamed for help. My father's mother came and bit the cord. 'My, Baba, what strong teeth you have!' Only six, but six good ones."

His tone is warm and playful.

"Soon all the relatives arrived, and everyone was toasting my future with swigs of plum brandy.

My mother wanted to christen me Spiro, which was the name of her dead brother. This didn't go over with the priest, a three-hundred-pound slab of meat with a voice as strong as the trumpet of the Archangel Michael. Father Bilbija licked my father's brandy off his lips and said it was wrong for a woman to choose the name. When no one spoke against the old fartmaker, he looked up at the calendar and said, 'The boy was born on the day of Saint Gabriel, and therefore he will be called Gavrilo.' Because of this, I think, my mother never protested much when I skipped Sunday Mass."

He lifts his eyebrows in a half-apologetic, half-so what? expression.

"I hated school almost as much as church, but I loved to read. Books on anarchy and socialism. Alexander Dumas, Oscar Wilde, and the exploits of Sherlock Holmes. My idol was Sima Pandurović, the poet. I read everything I could get my hands on. For me, books signified life. So it was very hard for me in prison, with nothing to read. I missed my books more than I missed my arm. I also wrote a little, but I wasn't very good, I confess. Roses blossoming for a lover at the bottom of the sea, that sort of thing. The last poem I wrote, I scratched on the soft walls of the Theresienstadt prison with a rusty spoon. A two-line poem, intended to spook the Austrians, whom, I believe, were given to superstition. I think I still remember it. Would you like to hear it?"

"Yes, I would."

He smiles slightly and looks at his feet. "Our ghosts will walk through Vienna / And roam through the palace, frightening the lords."

We sit in an odd silence together, watching clouds break on the cockpit window. A poet. This man I didn't know but still derided and, in my own way, hated.  A poet.  And a Sherlock Holmes fan, with those cool deductions and neat conclusions.  I didn't know, I couldn't have known, all this about him.

But.  He did it.  He killed a man, and his wife, and his chauffeur, killed people he had never met before, strangers, for nothing but *nationalism*.

"Why?"  I ask him, and I don't care that my voice ruptures this lovely little moment of ours.  "Why did you kill them?"  I want him to tell me, I'm dying for some wonderful, soothing logic, yes, that might cure what ails me.

He ignores my belligerence and answers calmly: "Mara, you will never understand."  He looks upset, perhaps with me for bringing it up, or maybe with himself.  Either way, his answer isn't good enough.

"Please, I must insist.  Explain to me why you did it."

He shakes his head, breathing audibly through his nose.  "The things you think about me, they're not true.  But I can't make you see.  You've never lived there.  You don't know.  What I did wasn't heroic.  And I'm sorry for the lost lives, especially the woman's.  But I'd do it all again, for my country."

The words "for my country" detonate something in the back of my brain.  "You pathetic thing.  You think everything's alright, everything's permissible and forgivable, as long as it's 'for my country.'"

"A country, when you don't have one to call your own, *is* everything.  For God's sake, we needed a home!"

I'm disgusted.  "You killed innocent people.  An unarmed woman and a chauffeur.  You coward!"

"Stop!" he shouts.  "You don't understand anything.  My country — "

"Fuck you and your pitiful little country!"

His fingers clamp around my wrist. "You've never had to fight for your identity. You take so many things for granted. You can't imagine — "

"Fuck you!" I scream, pulling my wrist back. "You're all monsters, all of you. There's nothing you wouldn't do for your stinking country. You'd cut the throats of babies and rape your babas and bite the balls off dirty street dogs."

His eyes pop out of their sockets, his mouth is open and nothing comes out, and I see the crooked black teeth, and then he shouts, "SHUT UP!"

He tears at my shirt, leaving me one sleeve and my bra exposed. He falls clumsily onto me, pushing me to the floor. He hits my chin, tries to shove my nose into my brain, his sharp thumb in my eye, and then he twists my breast, hits my nose again, fills my eyes with tears, I can barely see. He pulls up my skirts and feels me, *touches me*, he's laughing.

I push him away, and he flies off me. He bangs his mangy head on the control panel and a potted plant slips from the ledge and cracks him on the base of the skull. Then I'm on him, punching, and I stand up, he tries to shield his head, I kick him hard in the neck and he cries out, I kick him again and again until he stops begging, until his body stops flinching from the blows, until he is dead.

The plane's wheels touch down in Belgrade.

¤

# 15

September 26.

What a day!  I met Dave at By the Way after going to Karen's for my second lesson (that C chord is bugging me).  It was chilly out, so Dave and I had some hot apple cider.  Dave was nervous and jittery, it was funny how he could only look me in the eye for about two seconds before glancing away.  We talked about our families.  Dave's father owns a small construction company, where Dave's worked part-time the past two summers.  His mother stays home and takes care of the brood.  She cooks Irish stew nearly every night and tries valiantly to teach her children to play the piano, which none of them wants at all.  I can tell Dave really loves her a lot, the way his face brightens up when he talks about her.  He's the oldest kid, with three younger sisters who actually join together, hold him down and sit on his head if he treats any one of them badly.  I told him a little about my own family, too, even mentioning Nick, which surprised me, thinking of him as part of my family.  The weasel-lipped cretin is my *whole* family, now.  I think Dave found it all interesting, especially Danny, speculating on what he's like now, a ten year-old boy, wherever he is.

Krushalya, Ling Ling and a couple other guys joined us later.  No one wanted to divulge anything about where we were going. We headed over to Bathurst and then onto a dark sidestreet, Cecil or Cyril or some English uncle name like that. An old church leaned on the corner there, most of its stained-glass windows broken and graffiti spray-painted everywhere ("EURIPIDES PANTS, EUMENIDES PANTS"). It looked suicidal, if that's possible for a building.

I followed the gang down some steps and into a basement. People crowded together in a low-ceilinged room, lit only by dim blue spotlights. One older man wore a red hockey sweater, and when he turned around I saw that it wasn't a Montreal Canadiens jersey, which is what I assumed it would be, and it wasn't that other red team, the one with the great big Indian head. In fact, there was no emblem at all on this guy's jersey, just four letters sewn across the upper chest — C.C.C.P.

Ska music blared from some hidden speakers, "Tears of a Clown," by Krushalya's fave band, The Beat. A bunch of people started dancing in the space in front of the stage, and Krushalya elbowed her way to the middle of it all. She looks cool when she dances, so happy and energetic, hiking up her poncho and pumping one leg into the ground like she's stomping ants.

I was busy admiring Krushalya's technique when someone touched my arm. It was Dave, with a cup of beer for me. I said thanks and took it, and then he kissed me on the chin. The whole thing was very fast, and awkward. He looked embarrassed (was he aiming for my lips?), but I just smiled and drank the beer. I can't believe he kissed me like that, without any warning, but I'm glad he did. It must have been hard for him.

When the music stopped, a guy with badgers for sideburns climbed up on stage. He called us "comrades," which is when someone even as dense as me started to clue in. He gave a speech on atrocities in Chile. When he was finished, he introduced a band. Five guys — one in a wheelchair lifted onto the stage by the other four — began playing beautiful Chilean folk songs. One played the wooden flute, one a drum and the others strummed guitars. The songs were in Spanish, of course, with the wheelchair guy singing lead. When some couples started dancing during a slow song, Krushalya whispered in my ear to ask Dave to dance. I went over and took his hand and we danced.

Maybe it was the romantic music, or the beer, or the whole underground-type mood of the evening, but I began to feel close to Dave. He held me so lightly, up on my back like a perfect gentleman. I put my hand around his neck and pulled him nearer to me. I kissed him on the corner of his mouth, and then pressed my cheek against his. His skin felt smooth, and warm. We touched cheeks and swayed to the rhythm, until the song ended and a faster one started. Dave suggested we go outside for some fresh air.

We walked two blocks to a parkette and sat on a bench. We'd left our coats in the church and it was pretty cold out, so I slid over and asked Dave to put his arm around me (not subtle, I admit, but it got the job done). We gazed up at the stars together, and I don't care if that sounds corny. He stroked the back of my hand with his fingertips. I rested my head on his chest and wished we could be like that forever. Smelling his deodorant turned me on: pine trees. I really wanted him to kiss me again, but he didn't. So I kissed him.

Krushalya and the others found us, lugging our coats with them. A tall, orange-haired guy had his arm around Ling Ling. He looked familiar. When I spotted the scar above his temple, I realized it was my old enemy from grade school, Justin Eton-Edwards, covered in pink zits. He didn't recognize me.

We went to an all-night café on Queen. Dave and I had missed some slide-show on torture in Chile. Krushalya seemed distant, and when I asked her what was wrong she said she's worried about her mother, because her father had a mild heart attack two days ago. This other guy, Andy, wasn't too cheery, either, since he's getting evicted from his apartment. Overall, everyone was pretty down, and it took an effort for Dave and me not to smile at each other.

Over two years of masturbating, and I've never thought about someone I knew, it's always been some nebulous fantasy lover.

Not tonight.

¤

September 27.

Four-fourteen a.m., and David O'Malley sleeps in my bed. I can't believe it, I'm not a virgin anymore! I'm writing this by the hazy moonlight, I don't want the desklamp to wake him up. My hand is shaking like, SHIT!, never mind the similes, it's shaking, it's shaking! I'm sitting here wearing just a t-shirt, and my bum's sweating on the vinyl chair. I smell raunchy. I'm an overcharged battery, I want to swim and climb mountains and shoot skeets, and I'm not even sure what skeets are, birds, maybe, or tin cups? I don't know, I don't care.

Oh God, where to start. Just as I settled into my pre-sleep relaxation (see above), the phone rang. It's been ringing at night a lot lately, always for Nick.

After about twelve rings I answered it, and it was Dave.

"What's going on?" I asked, pleasantly surprised.

"Oh, I went home and couldn't sleep. It's a marvellous night, and I'm just around the corner at the donut shop. Do you want to come meet me?"

"Sure," I said. And then I thought about Nick: light bulb. "Why don't you come over? My uncle's gone," I said, not caring if it sounded like a come-on.

"Okay. I'll be right there."

I put on some jeans and my last clean t-shirt. As soon as I opened the door, I mashed my lips against his. He tasted sweet. He smiled and handed me something, a book by a poet he likes, Rachel Hadas (it's beside me right now, he said I could keep it). I kissed him again, and then I took his hand and led him to my room.

I felt so giddy I thought I'd laugh out loud. We sat down on the bed and necked. I could tell he didn't want to rush me, he was waiting for me to let him know it was alright. I eased him back on the bed and then unbuttoned his shirt, touching his chest, feeling his ribs (he's so thin!). We took nearly forever to get undressed, kissing passionately through it all, and when we finally got my shirt off I felt so horny that I wasn't thinking about how small my tits were but that I was going to share them with someone for the first time. He kissed my nipples; I unhooked his belt while he unzipped my jeans and pulled them to my knees, underwear, too. He put a finger inside me, saying it was all warm and gushy like the inside of a pumpkin (which he assured me is a compliment).

I pulled his pants off. There was already a wet stain on his underwear, which were being stretched considerably. I whipped them off and felt his cock, it was hard and straining, holding its breath. He kissed my stomach tenderly, the kindest, sexiest thing imaginable. Then he asked my permission(!) to make love to me, and I said yes, of course. He took a condom from his wallet and put it on. It looked funny, almost glow-in-the-dark. I leaned back and closed my eyes. He put it in, and it hurt, but only for a second, and then it felt great. I liked the feel of him on top of me. I liked him in me. I love his lips, his eyes, his thighs. His bent knees. I love the way he kisses my body everywhere.

We slept for an hour together before I woke up (a bad dream). He's so beautiful, look at him! I'm going back to lie down with him, I can't resist.

⌀

September 28.

Sunday night. I just re-read the last two entries, and I feel ashamed. Krushalya was going through a rough time and I barely noticed. I'm so selfish.

Yesterday morning (okay, early afternoon), Nick woke me up with a loud rap on my door. Nick is very fond of this manoeuvre. "Phone!" he shouted. "Phone for the lazy girl who sleeps all day!" I'd been dreaming all night about Dave, and I half-expected it to be him calling. (We saw *Casablanca* at The Bloor Cinema last night, and we both cried like saps at the end. No x-rated sex on this date, though, just good clean making-out in the park after the movie.)

"Hello," I said, with Nick three feet away from me, chapped lips smirking.

"Hi." It was Krushalya. She sighed. "I didn't wake you, did I?"

"Yes. No. Well, yes. What's up?"

I heard a low, muffled noise, like she was covering the receiver with her hand. "I made some vegetable curry. Want to come over for lunch?"

Krushalya rents a room on Humewood from these old-style hippies (tie-dyed shirts, weed, "man" at the end of every other sentence). I could smell the sweet mix of curry, cumin and marijuana even before the door opened.

Krushalya thanked me for coming and gave me a big hug. She looked awful, her hair messed up, eyes puffy and red. Even her poncho seemed extra creased, and she wore no tights beneath it, just her bare legs sticking out.

We went to her room. A single mattress lay on the wooden floor. Even without a carpet, the room felt cozy. Two skulls sat atop a dresser. The skulls were dirty, and looked real. (They are!) But Krushalya didn't want to explain them just then. She sat at the head of the mattress, against the far wall, and motioned for me to sit beside her. She tipped over in slow-motion, like a cowboy shot dead in a high-noon shoot-out. She buried her head in my lap.

I put my arms around her shoulders and asked her what happened.

"My father had a second heart attack. He's dead. My mom called. She wants me to live with her, says she can't even stand up, she's so upset."

"You can't do that," I said.

We laid down, our heads sharing the only pillow. Krushalya started crying, and she was in so much pain that I turned my head and caressed her chin and kissed her tear-stained cheek. For a long time we didn't say anything.

The house was quiet. The big window facing west framed the slow sunset. I thought Krushalya had fallen asleep, her breathing was heavy and even. All of a sudden, a sharp, angry peal of thunder exploded from nowhere.

I sat up and asked, "What was that?"

Krushalya laughed. "Jimmy next door. Lighting his cherry bombs. His uncle's a travelling salesman, gets them in the U.S. Stupid, jug-eared kid's going to blow off his little weeny before he ever gets a chance to use it."

My stomach grumbled loudly just then.

"Oh, Mara, I'm sorry," she said. "I forgot all about the curry. Let me go downstairs and warm it up."

In a couple of minutes she came back with a brown tray holding two plates of curried vegetables on a bed of rice. We sat cross-legged on the mattress, eating and talking. The food was delicious, and spicy. Krushalya asked me how things were going with Dave, and I told her I really liked him.

"Great," she said. "I figured you two would get along."

We finished eating and returned our plates to the tray. Krushalya's lips trembled, and she began crying again.

"I don't know what's wrong with me," she said, wiping the tears away. "I haven't cried in years."

"It's alright," I said, stroking her arm.

She snorkelled back some snot and said, "You must think I'm a mental case, going on like this after telling you how much I hate my dad."

"Not really."

"He used to beat me so much, Mara. Do you sleep in the raw?"

I was taken aback by the question. "Um, sometimes. If it's hot."

"Well, I have this thing against wearing pajamas; I like to be naked in my cool sheets. When I was little my mother bought me a thick, flannel nightgown. I hated it. It made me feel claustrophobic and strangled. I told my mother this, but she only shook her head and said that if my father found out I was sleeping in the nude, he'd kill me. But I just couldn't stop, I had to be naked."

"Let me guess: your father found out."

"Yeah. He whipped me good with that fake alligator belt of his. Cheap green shit. I felt sorry for my mom, really, because it hurt her more to watch than it did for me. She tried to stop him, but the big asshole just flicked her a nasty back-hander and she ran out of the room bawling."

"That sounds awful."

"The worst thing is that she made me wear that damn nightgown. Of course, my father checked the very next night. As predictable as a morning piss. When he saw that I was wearing it, he patted my head like I was a good little doggie who'd learned her lesson. After he left, I took my school scissors and cut out three holes, one for each breast and one for my crotch."

I smiled. "Did he catch you?"

"Not for a couple months, and then, surprise surprise, he whipped me again. But he did finally give up on getting me to wear anything to bed." She looked over at her dresser. "I noticed you looking at my skulls."

"Yeah," I laughed. "Never thought I'd hear that. Are they real?"

"What do you think, I'm going to have phony skulls in my room? Sure they're real. They're from Guyana. My mother and I worked on a garden when I was there, and we dug these up. They were attached to skeletons, of course. My mother went psycho, saying we should call the police, but my dad said no, it'd just cause trouble. He was right, too. The cops hate us Pakis. They're so racist, even though they suffered the same thing when the British were around."

"What are the cops?"

"Black, mostly. Anyway, my father, before he went to work the next day, told us to bury the dirty skeletons even deeper. When he left, my mother the chicken asked me to do it alone, and I did, after pulling the skulls off first. It was real easy, like plucking apples from a branch. Want to touch one?"

She carried them to the bed in a way that reminded me of how Valerie used to show me her new dolls. She placed one of the skulls in my palms.

"Smooth heads, don't you think? Good, strong craniums, can't go wrong with that," she said, knocking on the one she was holding. "Teeth are crooked, though. And rather unsightly overbites, I must say. In my opinion, these two were delinquent in their visits to the dentist."

"And you brought these through customs?"

Krushalya smiled. "It would've been great trying to get out of that jam."

It was dark by now. Krushalya lit a tall green candle and put an Animals record on. A moody version of the Rolling Stones' "Paint It Black" played first.

Krushalya took the tray downstairs and came back with a bottle of red wine. We drank straight from the bottle. It felt special, ceremonial somehow, like we were becoming blood-sisters because our lips shared the same bottle. We talked about music and stuff and eventually she got around to asking me if I'd done it with Dave yet. I thought she'd never ask...

"I knew it," she said, punching my shoulder. "Congratulations."

"Thanks."

"Well, I'm happy for both of you."

"He was my first," I said, looking at the flickering candle. I guess I felt a bit immature admitting this to Krushalya, she's been around more than I have.

Krushalya nodded and said, "Dave's a good guy to lose it with."

I laughed and felt up her knee. "How would you know?"

"Oh, nothing like that," she said. "But I can just tell. My first time, I was thirteen and the guy was seventeen. Sort of a prick, which I already knew, but I was curious and he was such a hot-looking beast that I didn't want to wait."

"Was it good?"

"As a learning experience. You know, touching a penis for the first time, and all that. But it's better with someone you like, middle-class as that sounds."

"Do you have a boyfriend now?"

"I don't really have boyfriends," she explained, sounding sad and proud at the same time. "I can't have attachments. I'm not lonely, though. I have my little stable of lovers. Mostly guys in the Y.C.L."

For some reason I blurted out, "Have you had any female lovers?"

She laughed out loud and stroked my cheek in a mock-sexy way. "Gee, Mara, you're not trying to seduce me, are you?"

"No, no," I said. "Sorry, I didn't mean to offend you or anything."

"Offend me? You think you're talking to a nun? The truth is, there have been a couple times. Want to hear about it, or would that gross you out?"

"No, it wouldn't gross me out."

"Well, the first time was two years ago with this girl I met at my old high school. Natalie. She looked like a cuter version of Janis Joplin, including the wire-rimmed glasses. We got into an intense conversation on communism one day. I said I had a great book on Che Guevara she should look at. She asked if she could come by and pick it up, and right then I knew. As soon as we got in the door, she kissed the nape of my neck."

"Wow. What was that like?"

"Different. But nice. We started Frenching. Her lips were so soft, not like any boy's I've ever kissed. She was a fast worker. She had her hand up my shirt and she was squeezing my breasts, and then we fell on the bed. She pulled off my tights and, ah, are you sure you want to hear about this?"

"Yeah," I said, not wanting to seem so eager but I couldn't help it.

"Well, she ate me out and made me come in about five minutes, despite the fact that she kept calling me her 'brown bunny.' Then she came back up and sucked my nipples. I figured it was my turn to go down on her, but I was nervous about it."

"You?" I said, pretending to be bowled over. "Nervous?"

"I'm not Cleopatra, you know! I get nervous, too. Natalie was such an expert, and I was a beginner. I was afraid I'd screw up. But I did it."

"And? What was it like?"

She made a funny face. "Bizarre, really. Almost narcissistic, like doing yourself. I didn't care for it. And the smell wasn't too appetizing, either."

"Gee," I laughed, "just like what the guys always say."

"Yeah. I have to resolve that dilemma."

"So," I said, not able to hold off teasing her, "didja get her off? Huh?"

She shot me an indignant look. "You serious? Me? Of course I did."

She stood up and flipped the record over. She never did get around to talking about the other time, and I wasn't about to ask for more details.

We sat there, drinking in silence, our backs against the wall, looking at the pale stars outside the window. Every time Krushalya handed me the wine after taking a swig, I put my lips gently to the bottle, like a kiss. It's strange to think about it twenty-four hours later, but I got turned on being with her, though I knew it was innocent.

She put another record on, something by Bessie Smith, all scratchy and soulful. When the side finished, Krushalya didn't make any move to change it. Neither of us was asleep, but we were both beat and drunk. The candle went "psst" and died.

"I think I should go home," I said, trying not to slur my speech.

Krushalya sat up so alertly she must have been on the verge of passing out cold. "Sleep here."

"On *this* bed?" I asked, not meaning to sound tactless or ungrateful.

"I'm not going to rape you," she said. "I'm too tired." She yanked off her poncho and flung it to the floor in one easy motion. She wore no bra, and her breasts swung from the effort. I was so drunk that I didn't realize I was staring. "You like 'em?" she asked, her eyes already closed for the night. Her head hit the pillow and she pulled me closer. I slept in her arms the whole night.

✖

October 4.

    Something's wrong. I went to Karen's for my lesson yesterday. I rang the bell. No answer. I went around back and looked in the window. She was lying in bed with a pillow on her head. She was breathing, so I left it at that.

    I came home and realized I hadn't seen Nick in a couple days. I'm sort of worried now. I have mixed feelings about the bum, but in general I think he's okay, and he does look out for me, maybe not like a parent, but considering the circumstances, I don't know, I think he's not so bad.

    I was getting ready to meet with Dave when I heard a knock at the door. No one ever knocks here, especially at night. Bad omen. Once I witnessed a wedding procession — happy, honking, paper-flower covered cars — held up at an intersection by a funeral procession, two dozen dark, sober cars passing so slowly it was sadistic, rubbing the newlyweds' noses in all that death.

    I opened the door. A burly man, whose jaw may have been wired shut, grunted "Nick." (Ah, brevity.) Though his arms were behind his back, he still conveyed menace: sweat on his brow, beer on his breath, hair on his nose.

    "He's not here," I said. "Can I take a message?"

    He took a step forward and glanced inside the apartment, giving me the impression that if he thought Nick was here, he would have shoved me aside and searched the joint. Luckily, he seemed to believe me; he walked away.

    I called Dave to cancel. I have to be alone when things fall apart.

◘

October 12.

It's been over a week.  There's been no word
from Nick.  I don't know where he is or if he's okay.  I
call Karen fifty times a day, but she won't answer,
assuming she's even home.  I missed four days of
school this week.  I went Friday; it rained.  Richard
brought in this moronic war story that first made me
laugh, then cry.  I read it at lunch in Fatso's, before
anyone joined me.  Called "Eight Days Till Midnight,"
it's about a butt-kickin', tobacco-spittin' American
spy (from "the future") who infiltrates K.G.B. head-
quarters and, when he's uncovered, goes on a manly
killing rampage in Red Square.  Jesus!  Glorified violence makes me sick, especially after seeing all that
stuff in Holocaust Studies.  Were it not for the black
electrical tape holding Richard's eyeglasses together
— I must admit, I do like the pathos of that — I'd
punch his face in.

Krushalya, it turned out, was the only one
who came for lunch, all long-faced and depressed.  I
hate to see her like this.  If someone as intelligent and
beautiful and brave as her can be sad, then what
chance is there for me.  She's fallen behind in school
(sounds familiar), and her mother's on some sort of
tranquilizers back in Guyana, calling Krushalya at all
hours with her "crazy talk."

"What do you mean?" I asked.

"Oh, she thinks my father's ghost is roaming the
halls.  One night he was an evil ghost seeking revenge,
although I couldn't guess for what.  Another time he
was a penitent ghost, begging forgiveness.  And last
night he was a hungry ghost, looking for chick peas."

"Chick peas?"

"My father's favorite."

I asked Krushalya if she'd seen Ling Ling lately.

She looked out the window and said, "Not since Monday."

"Do you know if she had her operation?"

"Oh, her eyelids?" she said, in a sarcastic tone. "She sure did."

"And? How does she look?"

"Surprised."

"Very funny."

"I don't mean to be flippant about it. Ling Ling and I had a big fight the day before she checked into the hospital."

"Don't tell me you bugged her about it again?"

"Bugged her?" she said, almost shouting. "It's insane! It's mutilation!"

The guys at the next booth stared at us a moment. I waited a bit before saying, more quietly, "It's her life, Krushalya. I know you care about her — "

"I do," she said, and she put her hand over her eyes. Although she may have been close to tears, she recovered fast and came back swinging. "I think Ling Ling may have done it for that prick she's seeing."

"Justin?"

"They're in love. What a joke."

The waitress came and Krushalya told her she didn't want anything.

"I saw you giving him some strange looks that night in the café."

"I used to know him," I said. "A long time ago."

"Lucky you," she said, stealing some of my fries.

"How'd he ever get involved in the Young Communist League?"

"He started hanging around a couple months ago. Probably heard that red chicks were easy." Her shoulders rose and fell. "The anglophile somehow impressed Ling Ling. White trousers. Quoting *Churchill*, as if anyone gives a shit. Drinking Earl Grey, eating scones. What torpor! Life's unfair, Mara."

"You really think Ling Ling did it for him?"

She crossed her arms on her chest and gave a dejected sigh. "If not for him, then for his kind."

That night, there was a demonstration at an aluminum factory in East York. A bunch of us from the Y.C.L. took the bus north to lend support. (Nick, who hates communism more than he does my cooking, would've ridiculed me forever if he found out.) The plant illegally locked out all its workers last month, and the shop steward (whose son, Ray, is in the Y.C.L.) thought it'd be good to have us there. Forty or so workers walked the picket line, with a dozen of us (Dave didn't show).

When nightfall came, the workers lit fires in big metal trash cans. We walked in front of the chain-link fence surrounding the factory. Around eight o'clock, this red Camaro pulled up and parked by the fence. Everyone stopped to watch (I figure because the monotonous, circular motion favored by strikers the world over makes just about any diversion welcome). The passenger door opened first, and even in the dark and at a distance I recognized Ling Ling's red windbreaker. The door opened on the driver's side and a long, white pant leg extended to the ground. Justin Eton-Edwards, Esq. Everyone, except for Krushalya and me, resumed the clockwise shuffle to nowhere.

Finally I understood why Krushalya was so upset with Ling Ling. From the time I first heard about it, I'd equated her operation with putting make-up on or wearing a new dress, just another change of looks. But now, up close, this was evil and macabre, sort of like *Invasion of the Bodysnatchers*. She looked different, otherworldly, more like the pod replica of Ling Ling than the original.

We said hi and acted coolly toward one another. Someone came over and handed picket signs to Ling Ling and Justin. Ling Ling heaved hers up on her shoulder, while Justin leaned on his. I debated inwardly over whether or not to comment on Ling Ling's new look — "Like your new eyes" — but before I could decide Justin smiled and said, "You're Mara Rustic, right?" I nodded. "I asked Ling Ling who you were when we met a couple weeks ago, but it didn't sink in until just now. We went to school together at Southwood."

"Yes, I think I remember," I said, with a not-too-genuine smile.

Ling Ling frowned at me for not being friendly. She probably thinks Krushalya told me to hate Justin. I could have told her about the swing incident ten years ago, but I don't come off much better than Justin in that one. (Odds and ends department: there was blood on Justin's chin from where he'd tried to scrape off a zit. I wonder if he bleeds this much when I'm not around.)

Just then a rock landed close to us, having been thrown from inside the fence. A shadow moved quickly across the factory rooftop and disappeared. Some of the workers got angry. Then a police car pulled up — no siren, but lights flashing — and stopped just short of the picket line. This made everyone even angrier, since the whole thing looked orchestrated now.

Another rock flew from the rooftop and struck the side of a burning trash can, causing a reverberating clang. Everyone turned to see what the two police officers sitting in their cruiser planned to do about this. The cops did nothing.

The workers huddled together and talked about climbing the fence and catching the rock-thrower, whom they suspected was a foreman they called "Banana Jerry" (I cannot even guess why).

Two more police cars arrived, and then two more. Ray called the Y.C.L. gang over and explained that there might be some trouble.

Justin asked, "What kind of trouble?"

"If anyone wants to leave," Ray said, diplomatically, "that's okay."

Justin looked at Ling Ling and said, "We don't need this, do we?"

Before Ling Ling answered, Krushalya said, "Just go home, rich boy."

Justin said, "Well, what's the point of all this? I don't want to wind up in jail for nothing."

"Let me tell you something," Krushalya said. She lowered her picket sign and let it rest against her thigh, and I knew something nasty was coming. "They can lock you up in jail, but they can't keep your face from breaking out."

A few people laughed (Justin's not very popular). I looked at Ling Ling and I felt sorry for her, she looked really anguished, not knowing what to do.

"Clever," Justin huffed. "But you still haven't told me why we're here."

"You wouldn't understand, Mr. Camaro, but there happens to be a need for strong unions in this country."

"Get to the point," Justin said, in that supercilious way of his.

"The *point*?" Krushalya repeated, gaining steam now. "The point is that for ages proletarians have been crapped on by fat, greedy bosses, capitalist pigs who snort that their workers need jobs to make a living when it's the bosses who make *their* livings off the workers' backs. Understand that? Slaves are sold only once, but proletarians have to sell themselves by the hour, and the one protection they have against further debasement is the union. Read your Marx, rich boy, it's all there. The union. The union. The union!"

When she finally ran out of breath, some of the workers who'd overheard actually clapped. Ray said, "Boy, Krushalya. You don't just get to the point, you beat the shit out of it once you get there." Justin walked away, and Ling Ling exchanged a look with Krushalya before she went with him.

The whole thing makes me sad. It seems anticlimactic to mention that the demonstration ended with nothing big. The cops told everyone to go home, and we did. The next day, Saturday, I stayed home and waited for news about Nick. And I couldn't reach Krushalya, Dave or Karen. Where is everyone?

¤

October 26.

I'm sick. I started working at the bookstore again. I'm going to have to ask John for an advance so I can pay the rent Friday. Karen finally answered her phone and told me not to expect Nick back. She said he's okay, but he's in some kind of serious trouble. She mentioned that he's going to try to mail me some money. I wanted to ask her about my guitar lessons, but from the tone of her voice I could tell that was history. Whatever Nick did really hurt her.

Speaking of men hurting women, I found out Dave's back together again with a girl he met in the summer. He's been avoiding me, not even showing up to writing class. When I called him last Saturday he acted weird and told me he'd have to switch to another line. Then, whispering, he told me "Elaine" was there. They'd had a hot summer fling before breaking up in September. Then, when he ran into her at a record store a few weeks ago, the sparks they flew.

I surprised myself by not breaking down and crying. It hurts, though. I thought I loved him. Krushalya's amazed I'm taking it so well. I guess I'd be more upset if this other junk weren't happening. Imagine not having time for a broken heart! Krushalya's kept me busy with the Y.C.L. I don't care much for all the reading she's "assigned" me (Marx, Lenin, yuck!), but I do like the people there. Krushalya's going through a rough time, too (her mother), so we're both trying to keep our minds occupied. I've been thinking of asking her to move in, since we spend so much time together anyway. I think we'd get along great.

November 1.

This is the end of my journal. No more talking to myself. I'm sixteen years old. Sweet. Birthday Thursday. Today's Saturday. Sunday morning, technically. I feel ridiculous. And alone. God, this isn't what I wanted.

In August, a thick, sticky morning where I felt the awful humidity in my nightmares, I awoke and found Mama in the bathtub, lying in water and blood. What a picture. What a poem. Written with a breadknife. A lifetime of agony captured in one final, pink moment.

After the initial shock — because no one wants to wake up first thing and find her lunatic mother naked and shrivelled and floating dead in the tub, when all she really wanted was to splash cold water on her face, and maybe take a piss — and that first spinning half hour, and after the ambulance attendants, and the policemen, and the nosy neighbors, after everyone had gone, I returned to my room and fell backwards onto my bed, arms stretched out blissfully, and I was laughing, I couldn't contain myself, I was laughing because it was over, I was free, of the madness and depression, getting my mother out of bed and dressing her and reading the Bible to her, feeding her, cooking, cleaning, and the late-night sobbing for her husband and son, the father and brother I wanted only to forget. Mama, I'm sorry. I am sorry. I miss you so much.

No, I deserve all this. I'm dirty. The tears rolling down my cheeks leave muddy tracks. Sounds like the beginning of an old blues ballad:

*The tears rollin' down my cheeks leave muddy tracks.*
*And I can cry all I want, they ain't never comin' back.*
*Please mister, please mister, I feel so black.*
*Shoot me in the field, and bury it in the grass.*

Mama's buried in a lovely green cemetery not far from here, about two miles away. The maintenance staff keeps the lawn neatly trimmed, I am told, and I'll go down someday to pay my respects. And maybe if I can find some I'll put two or three white roses on her grave, that would be nice. "Jelina Rustic," the tombstone probably reads. "Born May 1st, 1940. Died August 13th, 1980."

Lately I've been feeling like shit. School is a pit. Nick and Karen are both out of my life now.

(Nick did send a money order for eight months' rent, but the note said nothing about what's going on or if he's ever coming home, just "Hang in there, kid.") Dave is gone, too. I still see him, of course, but he's not there the way he was before. He looks vaguely embarrassed whenever I try to approach him. It's no use.

So here I am, the sad little orphan girl with no boyfriend, no uncle, no big-sister figure. A few days ago those things, as upsetting as they are, would not have mattered so much because I still had Krushalya. Now, that's over, too. It's all over. But before concluding this curse of a journal, I shall put to paper faithfully, to the best of my abilities (doesn't that sound formal and full of meaning?), the record of the end of my friendship with the kind-hearted and beautiful Krushalya Samad:

I'd been working a lot of nights recently, since I was unsure whether any money was forthcoming from Nick. Krushalya'd swing by the bookstore some of those evenings and walk me home. Friday night she came by with a strange look on her face, like someone who'd had a baby the same day she found out her house burned down. We walked for a while along Lakeshore. I kept asking her what was up, but she wouldn't tell me. She'd always been open with me, and I couldn't guess what'd make her hesitate to talk now.

We got here at about ten o'clock. Krushalya eased her backpack from her shoulders and took out a bottle of wine. We hadn't had anything to drink since the night she told me her father died, mainly because neither of us holds our liquor very well. When I asked her what the special occasion was, she said she wouldn't talk about it until all the wine was gone.

In my room, where I'd moved Nick's stereo and record collection, we listened to Van Morrison's mellow *Astral Weeks*. With the curtains drawn, I draped a purple t-shirt over my desklamp. We sat on the bed and drank in the dark violet, passing the bottle back and forth. Krushalya insisted on silence, shushing me every time I tried to speak.

As the bottle emptied, we started swaying into each other, clumsily, but with affection, first our knees touching, then elbows, before finally putting our arms around one another. Krushalya took a deep swig, looked me in the eye and whispered, "I love you." I cannot, I am not a good enough person or writer, I cannot quite describe the way I felt when I heard those words. A rush of warmth and happiness went straight to my heart, and I had tears in my eyes. Krushalya wiped them away with a tender finger, and I smiled and told her that I loved her, too. She smiled back and said, "I know."

When I asked her what the big news was that she didn't want to discuss, she told me it could wait until morning.

I got up and flipped the record over, and when I returned Krushalya was standing beside the bed. "Where are you going?" I asked.

"Do you mind if I sleep over? I really don't want to go home tonight."

"Sure. I'd like that."

She began undressing, and it was an effort for me to pretend I was engrossed with the album-cover art. After she crawled under the blanket, I grabbed my pajamas and headed for the bathroom to change. I felt like a big sucky prude. When I came back, Krushalya laughed and called me just that.

"Can I ask you for a favor, Mara?"

"Yeah?"

"Would you, um, feel uncomfortable sleeping in the nude with me?"

It took me a full five seconds to answer. "No, I guess not."

"I'm not being weird or anything."

"No, it's alright."

I took off my pajama top while Krushalya looked at me and grinned. I turned away from her to pull off the bottoms, and then, not wanting to even stop and think, I took off my underwear, too. Krushalya held the blanket up for me to come join her. I took a deep breath and climbed in. I laid there on my back for a couple minutes, looking petrified, I imagine, with the sheet pulled up to my neck and Krushalya propped up on her elbow, staring at me.

"What?" I asked.

"Nothing. I'm just looking at you. Don't be nervous."

"I'm not."

"Good."

She moved closer and put her hand on my cheek. Then she leaned in and gave my eyelids wet, lingering kisses.

I was rather enjoying this strange sensation, when Krushalya stopped. She laid her head against my chest and said, "Oh, Mara. I'm afraid to tell you."

"What is it?"

She sighed a few times. Then, "I'm leaving tomorrow for Guyana."

I thought about this a moment, trying to keep the panic away. I stroked her hair and said, "To visit your mother?"

"No. I'm going to live there."

This was the bullet. "Oh."

She didn't speak right away. When she saw that I wasn't going to say a thing, she asked, "Are you okay?"

"No."

She held me close, our bellies pressed warmly against each other. She kissed me on the lips, and put her hand gently on my breast. I moved my hand up and down her back, caressing her skin, it was so soft. We cried and made love, and in the morning she left me.

⋈

# 16

Mr. Pavić, attorney and gentleman, wants me to call him Zivko.

"*Dobar dan, Zivko,*" I say. "*Kako si?*"

Zivko smiles at my feeble Serbo-Croatian. "You speak very well, Mara."

"Thank you. *Hvala.*"

He shows me into his home and holds a cushy brown chair out for me at the dining room table. His slippers are ducks. That is unavoidable. A thing I could not avoid. The rest of his attire — a cool blue Italian suit, a matching silk tie, a buttoned-down shirt so immaculately white it makes me want to bathe — more than compensates for the yellow waterfowl hugging his feet: the overall effect is one of wealth and elegance. He sits down opposite me and begins, as if someone pressed PLAY on his mouth machine, to defend Serb army actions in a language I barely remember.

Zivko's grinning, non-stop wife, Jagoda, wears her long grey hair in a ponytail. She wipes the table thoroughly, scrubbing hard, like she's prepping for surgery. She leaves the room and returns with a plate of walnut-filled pastries rolled in icing sugar. Next, she serves us strong-smelling Turkish coffee in dainty, hand-painted cups sporting scenes from the Bible in black, gold and red. Zivko's cup features David hoisting Goliath's huge, blood-dripping head high above his own. Mine depicts the crucifixion under a big, golden sun. David and Jesus look like twins, the only difference being David's biceps are pronounced, while God's son apparently follows no work-out regimen.

Zivko switches to English when he notices my mind straying. "I am sorry for talking about this. Tell me, how was your airplane trip?"

"I slept through most of it."

"Good." He clears his throat and looks longingly at the crystal ashtray on the table. He calls to the kitchen: "*Molim Jagoda, donesi moje cigarete.*"

Jagoda brings him a pack of cigarettes. Even before handing it to him, she is wiping the table where he's spilled pastry crumbs.

"*Hvala,*" he says, returning her permanent smile without actually looking at her. He fumbles in his jacket pocket, pulls out a silver lighter, and lights his cigarette. After taking a few puffs, he asks, "Do you smoke?"

"No."

"Your father smoked very much. Two, three packs a day."

"Is that how he died? Lung cancer?"

"No," he says after a brief hesitation, as if he contemplated lying to me.

Jagoda brings me a tall glass of freshly-squeezed orange juice to wash down the Turkish coffee I have not touched. I say "*Hvala lepo*" and drink it, figuring that oranges don't grow on trees in Greater Serbia. She stands over my shoulder and watches me until the glass is half empty; satisfied, she leaves again for the kitchen.

The flimsy cloud of cigarette smoke winding itself slowly around Zivko's head gives him the haughty air of a café intellectual. He is about fifty-five years old, grey at the temples, quite handsome in a beefy sort of way, inexplicably tanned, with bushy dark eyebrows that nearly meet above a prominent nose.

I sip my orange juice and ask, "How did you know my father?"

"We had a friend in common," Zivko says after another hesitation, and I can't tell whether he's choosing his words so carefully because of his difficulties with English, or for another reason. He averts his eyes and adds, "That friend, too, is gone now. The three of us used to work in the same building."

He adds nothing more. I can see that he doesn't want me to pursue this line of questioning. Fine. "How did my father die?"

His wide face contorts into the dictionary definition of consternation, all frowns and twitches. Jagoda, who doesn't speak English, walks in with a bottle of *slivovitz* and two shot glasses pressed to her bosom. She places everything on the table with the clink-clink of glass colliding. She's about to pour when Zivko waves her off. "*Netreba*," he tells her. She picks up the three pieces and carries them back to the kitchen, her smile never waning.

"I don't mean to be rude, Mr. Pavić, but I'd like to know — "

"Please," he says, "call me Zivko. Your father was my best friend."

"Very well, Zivko. Please forgive me if I'm being ungracious. I just want to know what happened to my father."

He reaches for his second cigarette, shoves it in his mouth, and lights it. "Your father was murdered."

"What?" I say, not at all prepared for this (which, of course, begs the question, What the hell *am* I prepared for?). In my fantasies, stretching back like a lonesome desert highway over twenty years, my father gets killed over and over again in typical, everyday accidents: run over by a Dodge, drowned in a river, choking on a disagreeable lump of porridge, maybe crushed to death by industrial equipment in a factory with low safety standards. Something painful, yes, but ordinary just the same. Murdered? *My* father? Of all the possibilities, all the variations I played with in girlhood and adolescence while lying awake at night, murder is the one ending I never imagined.

"There was trouble on his street," Zivko says, after giving me what he must feel is enough time to absorb the news. "All the Croatian families were ordered off the premises. And they left, all except for one man and his wife. These people sent their sons to Zagreb, but they would not leave their home. They were," he says, closing his eyes to think of the word, "stubborn."

"Stubborn," I repeat stupidly.

He nods. "When it became clear that they were not going to leave, a man from the military handed your father a pistol and ordered him to kill these people, since they were his neighbors. Your father told the soldier, 'Never.' The soldier told him to think it over, and that he would be back the next day. Your father was advised by all his friends, and especially me, to do it. Those people were going to die, anyway. There was no reason for Tony to die, too."

"My father wouldn't kill them?"

"No. The soldier returned the next day with other soldiers. I was there. They gave your father one final chance. Next door, the Croatian couple shook like rabbits behind their curtains and watched. I begged your father to shoot those awful people. But he wouldn't. And the soldiers, they killed him."

I want to put my head in my hands, but this isn't the time for that. Instead I take a deep breath. "You said in your letter that my father left me something."

"Yes." He gets up and walks to the gigantic white china cabinet, looming over the table like a polar bear stuffed on its hind legs. He pulls a small brown parcel from the top drawer and holds it out to me with a sad look.

I take it and thank him. Then, "Where can I find my brother?"

He massages the lines on his forehead. "I'll give you his wife's address."

I thank him again and leave. We do not shake hands.

A cab had taken me directly from the airport to this house. I am now for the first time walking outdoors in Yugoslavia. The sun is shining.

⋈

# 17

Here I am, strolling through lovely downtown Belgrade. A swell opening line for a postcard. Close with, "P.S. I miss you terribly and wish you were here." Who would I write that to? Having finished reading my teen journal I'm thinking of Nick, a former Belgrade resident — "*Beograd*," he'd say. In the past few years I've heard from him more and more infrequently, skimpy envelopes out of the blue, never a return address. Somehow he's tracked me down through a dozen or so moves, even during my flirtation with university in Montréal. No paucity of eccentric postmarks, either: MEDICINE HAT, ALBERTA; EDNA, TEXAS; BONANZA, NICARAGUA. He's always cheerful ("Hey, kid!") and he still sends cash, although how he earns, or rather obtains, money remains a mystery to me. I wanted to write him, or even talk to him, but he never called, not once. Somehow I picture him hideously disfigured, courtesy of a knife fight with a guy named Lucas or Rico.

Everything here amazes me. The traffic lights: people obey them, the compact cars stop and start according to the normal red-green conventions. On the sidewalk, well-dressed pedestrians window-shop and laugh, not at all distressed by, say, the genocide and rape being carried out in their names.

From the main street, I pass two smaller ones and find the address I'm looking for. It's a modest, one-storey house, surrounded ominously by a black iron fence. I lift the latch on the gate. The hinges creak loudly; rust crumbles off in my fingers. I walk in and ease the gate gently back in place, fearful that a hard-enough push will bring the whole fence crashing down and wake the dead.

Closer, the house becomes less bleak. Three white lawn chairs take up space on the cluttered porch. Toys lie scattered about. It suddenly occurs to me that I may be an aunt. Aunt Mara. Crazy Tetka Mara. They'll make fun of me, I know it. And look over there, plastic dolls with big hair and stuffed pink creatures: they're girls' toys, that's worse, they'll notice the cracks right away.

I knock on the door, a good, solid door, oak perhaps, what do I know, fucking oak. I'm going to wake Edgar Allan Poe with my beating heart.

A black-haired woman holding a dishcloth opens the door. A pretty little girl hides behind her, tugging tenaciously on the woman's blue skirt. The mood is one of apprehension, even I can see that; they're expecting bad news.

The woman works a tired smile onto her face. After trying, and failing, to slap the girl loose from her dress, she nods almost imperceptibly and greets me warmly in her own language.

I smile and say, "*Dobar dan*," and then I ask her if she speaks English.

She turns her head and yells, "*Sestro!*" She smiles and steps back into the shadows of the hallway, taking the girl with her.

Another woman comes to the door, younger, without the smile. Like her sister, she has a strong chin and black, wavy hair. The sullen look on her face only intensifies when she is told I wish to speak to someone in English. She curls her lip at me and, with only the slightest trace of an accent, asks, "What do you want?"

"I'm sorry to disturb you. I'm looking for Danny Rustic's wife, Katya."

"That's me," she says, her voice uncertain now. "Who are you?"

A tickling sensation enters the back of my throat. This is my brother's wife. My sister-in-law. I feel a fog lifting from heart. After more than a decade, I'm looking a relative of mine in the eye. Katya's beautiful. Her hair comes down in delicate wisps over haunted green eyes. Her skin is pale, especially when set against the black sweater that hangs loosely on her thin body. She's my height, about twenty, twenty-one years old. "My name's Mara Rustic."

Suspicion creeps momentarily into her eyes, before her mouth, pouty and small, yet rebellious, softens into a smile. "Danilo's sister?"

She bursts out from the doorway and wraps her arms tightly around me. This unexpected kindness startles me so much that my eyes instantly well up with tears. Soon the household's other members — Katya's sister Jovanka and her daughter, Tina — join us on the porch for coffee and biscuits.

Katya says, "Incredible. The old lawyer told us about you in the summer, but we didn't believe him. You look like your brother, I can see the resemblance now, you have the same nose."

I'm only too happy to answer question after question about Canadian winters and what Danny was like as a baby (Katya laughs when I say "Danny," since he's always been "Danilo" to her). But after talking for almost an hour the conversation slows to a grim, heavy silence. Jovanka leaves with Tina to pick up another daughter from school. An unspoken sorrow exists between Katya and me. Like Zivko Pavić, she will not say where Danny is, what he is doing.

Katya asks, "Would you like more coffee?"

I shake my head no. I don't want to pressure her. Already, I feel close to her. I can sense her bravery in the way she bites the inside of her cheek and looks away when our eyes meet. The last thing I want to do is bring any more pain to her life. She loves Danny. She loves her Danilo. But I've waited so long, and I've come so far. "Where is my brother?"

She closes her eyes. "He's in Gorjemesto."

The name sounds familiar. I've heard it on the radio before, or perhaps read of it in the newspapers. "Is that in Serbia?"

It's in Croatia," she says, quietly. She opens her eyes and looks at me. "When Danilo received an offer to teach two years ago, we moved to a Serbian town near the border. Everything was going well. We were married a year ago last June."

She holds her hand up to show me the ring. An odd exchange of weak smiles.

Katya covers the ring with her other hand and continues. "The army — the Serbs in Croatia — began recruiting men, everyone who could walk, some who couldn't. Danilo didn't want to fight. He tried to explain to these soldiers that he was Yugoslavian, not Serbian, and that he refused to go to war against other Yugoslavs. Our friends were mixed, Mara: Serbs, Croats, Slovenes, even Muslims. We tried telling this to the idiot soldiers, but they only threatened to kill him if he didn't join. When Danilo told them to go ahead and shoot, they said they would kill me, too. And that's when he left with them."

I think of a coffin in Gorjemesto, and I cannot bear it. "Is he dead?"

A look of horror: "Oh, Mara, I'm sorry." She gets halfway out of her chair and hugs me. "No, Danilo's not dead. I'm sorry to make you think that."

My heartbeat returns to normal.

Katya sits down again. She picks up her cup and cradles it in her lap. "We made a mistake, Danilo and I. We thought he'd be exempt because of his teaching. His students loved him. His boys won the soccer championship last year. None of it mattered. They dragged him off in broad daylight. I came here to live with my sister's family. Then Danilo's father — "she catches herself" — your father was killed. Danilo took it badly. He wrote to me, said he'd take his own life before any soldier did. He said they were trying to make him do things, things he would never do. He's a sweet man, Mara. He's not a soldier."

She sweeps hair from her eyes and waits for a slow-moving, bent-over old woman to walk by on the sidewalk in front of the house.

"He stopped writing five months ago. I didn't know where he was, if he was alive, nothing. Six weeks ago I got a letter from a nurse in Gorjemesto. She told me he was in a hospital bed and that he wouldn't eat or sleep. I wrote him many letters, I even told him about you, that Zivko had found a sister in Canada. I thought it might raise his spirits. I told him I missed him. I told him I loved him," she says, looking into her cup. "But I didn't hear anything for a long time. Finally, the nurse wrote me back herself, saying Danilo wouldn't read my letters."

"Did you go see him?"

I feel ashamed as soon as the words leave my lips. Katya lowers her head and speaks in a whisper. "No. Crossing borders is forbidden. I thought of it, of course.  But I was afraid.  And I had no one I could ask to go with me."

"Katya," I say, and before I say anything else, we both know.

⋈

# 18

The next day, an overcast, windy Monday, Katya and I get up early and walk to the bus station. After a restless night in a room with Jovanka's daughters (they shared a bed to accommodate me), the cool morning breeze on my face invigorates me. This long, quiet walk with Katya is just what I need.

Jovanka's husband, Slobodan, had offered to give us a ride in the colorless Volkswagen Beetle his father's been driving since the glory days of Tito. Katya thought about it, and declined. Gasoline is rationed and very expensive. Slobodan looked relieved.

Late last night, Jovanka brought out a map and showed us the best route available. First we'll take the bus to Novi Selo, the town Katya and Danny lived in up until last March. Then, either by sneaking across or bribing whomever controls the border, we'll try to negotiate our way into Croatia. From there, it's about ten miles to Gorjemesto.

At first, Slobodan scoffed at our plan. When he realized how determined we were to see it through, he urged us in a very earnest, almost touching, tone to reconsider. He didn't have to spell out what might await us.

Katya and I make decent time and get to the bus station by nine o'clock. We sit in silence in the grey waiting area. She pulls from her inside coat

pocket a tattered copy of George Eliot's *The Mill on
the Floss*. She asks me if I mind. I smile and say no, I
don't. She says she's reading it for an English litera-
ture class she's enrolled in. (Poor Maggie and Tom,
brother and sister, die together in a flood; that much I
remember.) Once immersed in the book, the tip of
her tongue peeks out between her lips, an anchor to
her concentration. The pages turn quickly. Me, I'm
writing to you in my book of madness. The ink in my
pen is running out. We have an hour to wait.

Before we went to bed last night, Katya
showed me her photo albums. I saw pictures of
Danny at all the different stages of his life. (Weird,
like seeing one of those missing children computer-
graphic enhancements, illustrating what the kid
might look like today.) Danny's metabolism problem,
the profuse and unprovoked sweating, evidently con-
tinued until at least the start of high school. All his
school portraits — artless mugshots, really, just like in
North America — are notable for the perspiration-
soaked forehead and the damp, greasy hair. In his
teens he was thin and gawky, all elbows and knees,
and big ears poked out from behind a bad haircut I
recognized at once as my father's handiwork (my
mother didn't trust herself with sharp instruments).

Katya beamed when we got to the wedding
pictures. She wore her grandmother's beautiful old
gown, with a train as long as a swimming pool.
Danny, in his black tuxedo, looked handsome and
confident, the adolescent awkwardness gone. My
father was in the pictures, too, a spent ghost staring
back at me. It shocked me to see him like that, the
same man but not, older, grey-haired, stooped, weak-
er. Imagine finding the devil in a retirement home:
horns worn away, tail limp, pitchfork too heavy to
carry anymore and cream of mushroom soup drib-

bling down his lips. Do you call upon the armies of God to smite him down, or do you wipe his chin for him? After a few more pictures of him — making toasts, kissing Katya, standing between the happy couple with tears in his eyes — the shock wore off, and I began to see my father for what he was, a very average man, proud of his son and new daughter-in-law on their wedding day. And, at the end, a hero.

Katya told me about him reluctantly, since she could probably see the turmoil in my eyes as I thumbed through the album. My father was a janitor in a legal building, which is where he met Zivko. The two men were inseparable, drinking home-made wine together on weekends, playing games of chess for cigarettes, my father enthralling his friend with tales of the New World. When Danny reached the age when such things are considered, Zivko encouraged him to become a lawyer. Katya said my father was all for it, but Danny was set on working with children, either as a teacher or a pediatrician. Teaching won out when Danny's marks failed to meet medical school standards.

All this information, this instant history, is hard for me to absorb. It's too much to fit into my brain at once. I've decided not to open the parcel that Zivko gave me, at least until after I see Danny. I'm worried that whatever it is, it will upset me tremendously.

¤

Our bus lumbers into the station, announcing itself with the shriek of a sharp left turn. Fifteen passengers and a baggy-panted driver climb out. They look exhausted, like they just finished a double-shift down in a mine.

Katya says the driver will freshen up and in a few minutes we'll be off. Her voice, so small in the echo-filled station, reminds me that this is my idea. She's a child. Although she's dying to see Danny, I know that if it weren't for me she'd be safe at home right now, typing an essay for school. She's twenty-two years old, a year younger than Danny. The realization that I'm the "adult" here — chronology-wise, anyway — fills me with a dread and responsibility I've never felt before. I want to ask her if she's certain she wants to do this. But if I do, she'll be insulted; she wants this as much as I do.

On the bus, Katya lets me have the window seat. "You're the guest in this country," she says. In fact, there are no windows. Katya explains that all the panes have been removed as a precaution against sniper fire.

Within twenty minutes the bus leaves Belgrade's city limits, and there's a swift drop in the quality of the road; we're in the rural regions now. Despite the chilly, late-autumn afternoon, the farmers have their sheep and cows grazing in the pastures. All the cows seem ludicrously skinny to me, malnourished, even. When I point this out to Katya, she gives me a funny look, like it's impolite to notice such a thing.

After more than three hours of bump-ta-bump-ta-bump on primitive back roads the bus stops at its final destination, Novi Selo. Katya and I are the only ones left, the thirty or so other passengers having disembarked at earlier stops. It's just past two o'clock. There's no station here. The driver says it was blown up two months ago, by which side nobody knows for sure. He waves goodbye and pulls the door shut from the inside. He leaves us in the middle of nowhere.

Once the cacophony of the bus dies in the distance, the change in Katya is visible. She's thinking
about the times she and Danny shared in this town.
She stands on the road and spins a slow circle, looking all around her before facing me again. "This
way," she says, without much conviction.

We cut across an abandoned field and walk
towards the Croatian border. Reddish-brown, dried-
up stalks snap loudly beneath our feet. I find it hard
to believe this big chunk of nothing was once a
vibrant cornfield. We trudge into it dutifully, no com-
plaining, our arms held up to deflect the sharp sting
of dead and brittle vegetation on our faces. The map
is in Katya's hands. I follow her.

Katya's lugging a bulky knapsack, probably
filled with treats for Danny. I'm carrying a light
overnight bag, and beginning to feel guilty. After a
while, I ask her if she wants to switch. She doesn't
respond, and when I ask her again she shakes her
head no without turning around.

How strange this is, walking the old country
with a sister-in-law I met yesterday. Getting to know
her now would be difficult; everything is tainted by
this war. You hear inspirational stories about people
returning to their ancestral homelands and finding
some measure of, I don't know, peace, self-knowl-
edge, something. Look at this. I'm with an intelligent, warm-hearted young woman, and I can't even
have a normal conversation with her. Can't ask her
about her studies, about the music she listens to,
whether she's travelled much in her life, nothing. In
this backdrop, small talk is obscene.

We're about halfway into this enormous field
— a mile behind us, a mile ahead of us — when
Katya stops without warning. I bang into her knapsack, nearly sending us both tumbling to the ground.

Katya doesn't speak. I step around her to see what's wrong. There, on the ground, partially hidden by the weeds and cornstalks, lies a pile of dead babies, heaped naked on top of one another, five, seven, ten of them. Some look like newborns, others could be two years old. All of their tiny skulls are dented in. Flies and maggots feast on the soft baby flesh.

Katya puts her hand to her mouth and points to a copper-headed mallet lying nearby, blood-stained. She falls to her knees and throws up. I bend over her and clasp my arms around her back.

Afterwards, neither of us says a thing. I wonder, though. Were they rape babies? Or did someone see a star in the east?

¤

We emerge from the field onto a barren strip of highway, brushing burrs from each other's hair and clothing. It looks like rain. There's a checkpoint up ahead, fifty yards from us. Katya says it's Serbian, she can tell by the torn flag draped over the low roof. Tucked securely in the side pocket of her knapsack are papers proving Katya was born in Belgrade. Slobodan warned us that this identification might not be enough, that the soldiers might take one look at us and decide we weren't Serbs at all. Katya, however, thinks the papers, plus a bit of money (especially my American dollars), will be enough.

In the end, it doesn't matter. No one's manning the tin-shack checkpoint, which happens to be riddled with golfball-sized bullet holes. So is the portable out-house twenty feet behind it. These guys play for keeps. Katya and I look at each other and actually smile. We walk across the border and, just like that, we're in Croatia. We're too fast, and the coyotes are sleeping.

The sun makes a surprise appearance. Unfathomable to me, that it's the same sun the world over, that kids in Toronto play road hockey beneath it, and that wealthy tourists in Monaco smear sunscreen against it. We take off our coats and wipe our brows. Krushalya says we'll be in Gorjemesto in two hours.

I'm tired. Did Krushalya say that? No, Katya. Everything's so bright. I think I see her in the distance. A speck of blue on the horizon. The air hangs dense and hazy, mirage-making. We're walking towards her. What will I do? I can't tell Katya what I see, I can't be insane now.

My God, Gorjemesto! I finally make the connection; I *have* read about it. The Burning Village. It's the place those children see the Virgin. I feel relieved and, in a way, vindicated. The visions I had as a child stopped after my father went away. In an effort to recapture the visions of, I guess it must have been, Mary, I used to light fires in the wastebasket in my room and gaze into it, trying to bring her back. There were times when I thought I saw her in the flame, the blue in the orange and red, and once I burned myself reaching out to touch her; but it wasn't her. She never came again. By the time I was ten or twelve, I'd convinced myself that I'd hallucinated it all.

I tap Katya on the shoulder and say, "Look over there." But when we look, she's no longer there.

"What was it?"

I'm confused. "Katya," I say, looking to the left and the right, "isn't this place — Gorjemesto — isn't this the place people see Mary?"

She shoots me a sideways glance and keeps walking. "The Catholics believe it, if that's what you mean. Some kids say they've been seeing her for years. Why do you ask?"

I keep my head down and follow her.

At the outskirts of Gorjemesto, it dawns on me that we are in a Croatian zone. We've crossed sides, like in an espionage thriller. Katya asks the first person we see, a woman walking up the grassy hill we're descending, where the hospital is. The woman, covered by so many layers of rags she could be my age or a hundred, mutters something unintelligible and never breaks stride.

We go forward, to the more inhabited parts of the village. On one street, the remnants of a Catholic church and a mosque lie opposite each other, both buildings burned to the ground. In the soot and shattered glass of the mosque, a blonde-haired boy picks through the rubble. His legs straddle a bench and a tipped-over, blackened minaret. Katya walks over and asks about the hospital.

"*Tamo je bolnica*," he says, pointing beyond a conspicuous (because they're standing) group of one-storey houses, huddled together as if out of fear. Katya thanks him. She waves me over and asks me to pull a pear out of her knapsack for the boy. "Voliš kruške?" she asks him.

The boy says yes, and I drop a fresh pear into his small, dirty hands. In fact, Katya's knapsack is packed full of fruit, and I feel like a thoughtless pig for not bringing anything myself.

We arrive at the hospital. I had thought, as anyone might when hearing the word, that "hospital" implied a clean, sterilized medical facility with doors, windows and an intact roof. This isn't a hospital; it's a hurricane site.

About fifty feet from the main entrance (that is, the biggest hole in the building), Katya rushes wildly ahead of me and goes in. I follow her in a half-trot. She spots a haggard-looking doctor leaning back in a chair, eyes closed and arms folded behind her head. Katya, panting, asks the doctor about Nurse Lovic, the one who wrote to her about Danny.

The doctor opens her eyes. Bloodshot. She informs us, in a hoarse whisper, that the nurse we're looking for is in the cafeteria.

Katya asks if Nurse Lovic is eating dinner.

The doctor grins knowingly and tells us Nurse Lovic is *making* dinner.

Bugs fly everywhere in the cafeteria. It's a large, cold room. Sparrows make their way in through the holes in the roof. At the far end of the room, a nurse stirs a giant pot of soup cooking over a fire. The soup doesn't smell.

Nurse Lovic is nothing like I pictured her: I'd imagined big and sturdy; she's barely five feet tall, and bone-thin. Katya speaks with the nurse in their own language, and the tears that quickly form in her green eyes sink my heart. The nurse nods sympathetically and goes on in a caring tone, stirring the pot with a long wooden spoon as she speaks. Her speech is loaded with medical and military terminology, and though I hurt my head trying, I cannot follow what she's saying.

Katya thanks the nurse. She motions for me to go outside with her. We sit on the steps leading into the cafeteria. "Mara," she says with a despondent sigh, "Danilo's been in a coma for a few weeks now. It doesn't look good."

I bow my head, focus my eyes on a red stain on the ground, and try to brace myself. "Can we see him?" I ask.

"The nurse will take us to his room when she's finished making dinner. She told me what happened, how Danilo came to be here. She was afraid to tell me in a letter; she thought someone, our side or hers, would censor it."

She pauses, sticks her head between her knees, and lets out a moan.

"It's bad. Very bad."

I cannot look away from the stain, nor can I close my eyes. "Tell me."

She lifts her head. Out of the corner of my eye I see a sparrow hopping on the ground in front of us. "They took Danilo to Sarajevo. He was posted up in the hills with the Bosnian Serbs there. I don't know if I can tell you this. No, I can't," she says, her voice breaking.

The sparrow claws at the red stain. "Tell me."

Katya waits a moment. Then, "The nurse told me the Serbs in Sarajevo were decapitating people with chainsaws. One morning, a commanding officer sent an entire unit into one house. He ordered Danilo to execute the family. I don't know if I can say this. Danilo had a gun held to his head. The officer said he'd shoot him if he didn't obey."

Stop, I want to say. Stop, stop, stop.

Katya's crying now; I can hear the tears hitting the ground like raindrops at the start of a storm. "Danilo killed the father. Then the mother and the older child. When it was the younger child's turn, something came over him, and he turned and charged at the commanding officer, plunging the chainsaw into his belly. Before the other soldiers could react, Danilo took the child, a nine-year-old Muslim girl, and escaped. Six days later, they arrived here together."

This can't be. When I speak again, it feels as if someone injected a fat dose of novocaine in my lips. "What happened to the girl?"

Katya doesn't say anything for a while. The sparrow pokes its beak in and out of empty paper cups. "The nurse said Danilo and the girl were taken care of here. Both were sedated. But the girl, whom they thought was in a state of shock, vanished one night. She got out of bed, found the clothes she had been brought in, and walked out. No one knows what happened to her."

We go back into the cafeteria. Nurse Lovic finishes ladling the odorless brown soup into brown plastic bowls. We help her load the cart with the trays. Danny's room is not the first on her rounds, so we have to wait while others are served their meals. It seems, to my untrained eye, that many of the patients have no physical wounds. When I mention this to Nurse Lovic, she proceeds to give me a running commentary on the patients.

This man found his four year-old son blown to bits by a mortar round; he was found trying to piece together the dead boy's body, thinking it might bring the child back to life.

That young woman, a Muslim, had a good-looking Serb fiancé before the war; now that he's on the other side, she thinks that he is stalking her, slinking murderously behind every corner, and she has a burning sensation in her back to prove it.

That girl came home from school one day to find her mother being raped by soldiers; when the mother begged her attackers not to do it in front of her daughter, they laughed and sat the girl down in the middle of the room, where she witnessed her mother being beaten to death.

Nurse Lovic says the patients are, for the most part, harmless, staring glassy-eyed all day long at nothing in particular. Many of them no longer flinch when the bombs land and the hospital trembles like a wet dog left out in the cold. She tells us this is what Danny was like, before the coma.

The next room is Danny's. The large policeman guarding the door sits in a straight-backed chair with a look of rancor on his face. A recently-polished revolver rests in his hand. For just a second the gun frightens me, and then I almost laugh: in all my years living in Canada, I've never come face-to-face with a gun. Here, it must be commonplace, even for the youngest child.

When Katya and I try to pass into the room (following Nurse Lovic), the policeman stands. He's about to bar us from entering when Nurse Lovic snorts and says, "*Familija!*"

We walk into Danny's room, or rather, the room he is in. My brother shares cramped quarters with five others — three men, one woman, and one burn victim wrapped up so completely that I can't tell. The thick stench of overflowing bedpans is suffocating, an assault on the nose, the eyes and the stomach. I look around the room a second time, and am embarrassed to say that I don't know my brother.

Katya knows. She goes to her husband and reaches out for the bare arm hanging over the side of the narrow bed. She pulls back and looks at the nurse, whose nod tells her it's alright to touch him. She caresses his arm, and then takes his hand in hers, rubbing his fingers against her cheek.

He's my little brother. I walk to the other side of the bed. His eyes are closed. Flies swarm his head. He doesn't look at all like the pictures Katya showed me just yesterday. He's rotted away. His arms, in the sleeveless blue hospital pajamas, are white and spindly; his fingers are crooked yellow pencils. Even his bearded face, ostensibly at rest, is twisted into a grotesque, agonized smile. Danny. The handsome young man in the wedding pictures. My father was right, it's all luck, look what bad luck did to my little brother. But I can't. My arms are stuck at my sides. I can't. I cannot touch him. I cannot connect this man — this unconscious, hairy killer with the weird, shiny grease on his forehead — I cannot connect this man to the baby who used to lick my nose.

This is not my brother.

When Katya throws her head on his chest and begins sobbing loudly, I feel like an intruder. I step out of the room.

The policeman looks up at the click of the door opening. He gives me a look of unblemished hatred and tightens his grip around the gun. *Hello, I know you, you're related to the Serb madman; he's my enemy, and so are you.*

I walk quickly down the long corridor and arrive at an unexpected exit. I peek outside and see a vacant courtyard. The debris-filled lawn is surrounded on all sides by dilapidated hospital walls.

Behind me, I see the policeman advancing rapidly, my heart a magnet to his gun, held high and leading the way. *Hello.* Every angry footstep pounds a rivet into the floor.

I go into the yard. It's bright outside. I scramble along the peeling walls, thinking there may be another doorway I can pass through; there is nothing.

The policeman walks into the courtyard.

"I'm not from here," I say, too quietly to be heard. "I want to go home." I fall to my knees and keep my eyes lowered.

In a few seconds the policeman's shoes trample the grass and garbage directly in front of me. *Hello.* Without looking up, I know the gun is aimed at my heart. I stare at the ground.

I wait.

Smoke rises from beneath his shoes. And then more smoke, and more, until he himself notices and moves his feet. In the cleared-out piece of earth he has revealed, a tiny spark appears. The spark erupts into a huge flame, rising a hundred feet in the air and spanning the width of the entire courtyard.

Through the orange and red, I see him step back slowly in wide-eyed astonishment. He turns on his heels and runs back into the hospital.

In the orange and red, I see the blue.

⋈

# 19

We make it back across the border easily without incident.  Although my plane ticket has an open return date, I want to leave as soon as possible.  Katya understands.

When we arrive at the bus "place" in Novi Selo, Katya asks me if I'd like to go into town with her.  It's still early, and she wants to take me to the café she and Danny once frequented.  "They have very good sangria," she says.

Well, red wine laced with sugar and assorted fruits just might hit the spot right now, so I agree to join her.

We walk into town.  In the past few days I've racked up more mileage on my feet than I have in the past ten years.  I don't mind it here.  The people, the buildings, even the dogs and cats of Novi Selo, seem sleepy and peaceful.  I can see how Katya and Danny could have been happy here.  Katya says she will not forget him, that she'll wait forever, if necessary.

We drink the sangria.  Katya asks me if I've opened the parcel my father left me.  I tell her I haven't, that it's still in my overnight bag.  She nods and closes her eyes.

Just as we finish the tall pitcher — it was quite tasty — Katya spots a boy walking alone on the sidewalk outside.  She bangs hard on the window with her fist (the waiter gives us a nasty look). The boy sees Katya, runs into the café, and hugs her.

His name is Alex. He's wearing a green and black striped t-shirt with number seven on the back, black shorts with matching knee-high socks, and clicking cleats. He's full of energy, shuffling his small but stocky frame back and forth on his feet, the spikes scratching the café floor (another nasty look from you-know-who). Katya says Alex was Danny's favorite pupil when he was teaching. Alex blushes when he hears this, and Katya messes up his hair for him. There's a bright, puckish quality about this boy; I find myself unable to wipe the smile off my face. I can just see him hiding under a younger sister's bed at night, waiting for her to fall asleep, and then making scary, deep-voiced, I'm-going-to-get-you monster noises. And when his bleary-eyed parents show up in their nightgowns to investigate the ruckus, he charms his way out of a spanking, too.

Katya asks him how his soccer team is doing. He shrugs half-heartedly, looks down and doesn't say anything, and Katya and I both laugh.

An enthusiastic smile splashes onto his round face when he suddenly remembers something. He tells us his team, the one Danny coached last year, is playing this afternoon. He's on his way to the stadium now and he wants to know if we'll come and watch him. The idea excites Katya, but she waits for me to answer.

I say yes.

It's a beautiful day. The sun is out again. Alex walks between Katya and me, holding our hands while coaxing a speedier pace out of us.

At the stadium, Alex leaves us for the dressing room. Katya and I climb into the stands and see that the playing field is muddy from the previous day's rain. The stands are packed with the classmates and parents of the players, some of whom are loosening up on the sidelines with deep knee bends. Katya points out Alex, number seven, who stops doing the warm-up exercises every time his coach looks away. He's easily the shortest player on the team, though he's more robust-looking than most of the others.

The referee blows the whistle, and the game begins. Alex is almost lost in the crush of jerseys, dwarfed by the bigger players who elbow him aside for the ball.

After a while my mind wanders to other things. What day is it? I decide to open my father's parcel. In the crowded stands, a bunch of black and white photographs spill into my lap. The pictures are of my parents, of Danny, and of me. In one of them, I'm sitting in the park holding Danny in my arms. There is a big black dog sniffing around in the background. I show the photo to Katya, and she nods.

In the final picture, my mother is posing alone in front of a glaring statue, a general, perhaps. It had to be taken in Yugoslavia, she looks so young, only eighteen or twenty. Her eyes are hopeful.

I look in the envelope for anything else, and see that a single sheet of paper is stuck at the bottom. I scoop it out. It's written in a shaky, old man's handwriting. It's in English. "When we were young."

A small tremor rushes through the crowd, and some of the people close by stand up. Katya nudges me in the ribs and says, "Look! Number seven! Breakaway!"

We both stand. Alex is racing towards the other team's net, with no one between him and the goaltender. He's smiling from ear to ear. A few strides back, a much taller defender unleashes his long legs and gains ground on him.

Alex runs steadily, if unspectacularly, onward. The goaltender, crouched and ready to pounce, edges out of the net for a better angle. The defender has almost caught up to Alex by now, and people are yelling for him to shoot before it's too late, even Katya shouts for him to kick the ball, and this looks like what Alex intends to do, except at the last moment he's tripped up. His knees give out and he stumbles, and he's going to land on his face, but from behind him the defender pokes his foot between Alex's buckling legs and chips the ball up into the air. The ball flies up, eludes the lunging goaltender's grasp, and comes down in the net, lost in the mesh.

Number seven, arms raised jubilantly skyward, is mobbed by his happy teammates, who slap his back and help him brush the mud off his shorts.

Katya and I turn and embrace one another. The warm autumn sun feels good on my face.